The September Project

DENISE
M. JONES

Other Books by Denise M. Jones

Montgomery's Diary
Ned Finally Died

Thank you for the purchase of this book :)

The September Project by Denise M. Jones Published by Tis Swift

Visit the author's website at: www.denisemarquithjones.com

© 2020 Denise M. Jones

Paperback ISBN: 978-1-7341318-4-0

Cover by Deranged Doctor Design.
Edits by Jennie Allred (AllRediting)

First Edition

To the Women That Raised Me

Your task is not to seek for love, but merely to seek and find all the barriers within yourself that you have built against it.

−Rumi

We delight in the beauty of the butterfly, but rarely admit the changes it has gone through to achieve that beauty.

−Maya Angelou

Chapter 1

Cashmere

Cashmere Watson had a death wish. Waiting for the filming crew to pack up for the night had been tiresome but worth it just for the moment she snuck into Porchia's room.

Effective today, Cashmere was backing out of the deal she'd made with Emory. If she was being honest with herself, she'd known the agreement was null the moment she came onto the show. In the anatomy of reality show casting she was the new exciting wild card of 'curvy girl'. She should've represented the happy jolly 'I'm so excited just to be here' fat girl. The girl grateful for the bone tossed her way; a chance at the handsome bachelor. Every girl's fantasy…

Instead she gave the show its second vixen.

Cashmere had become the resident mean girl without a group backing her. The film crew had a nickname for her, the rogue one, which had nothing to do with the new Star Wars film.

She crept across the expansive room, the winner's luxury suite, drenched in white and oak. The large dresser and fancy ottoman to the right of her, the moment she stepped into the room. The sliding doors were open letting in the cool night air. It carried scents of smoke and sex.

Cashmere hadn't wanted to look past the ottoman to her left, the California King bed lay flush against the wall. She fought the memory of the fantasy she'd had about the room not so long ago. The trajectory of two bodies moving from one piece of furniture to another as untamed desire gave way to a whirlwind of pent up energy. She smiled remembering thinking about how they'd eventually make it to the bed... where nothing happened. It all came to an abrupt stop.

Cashmere shook her head, stuffing the emotions and fantasies down in a place as far as it could go. She wouldn't be bothered with distractions; she had one goal in mind. This goal was her primary focus but when she entered the room, she hadn't expected to find Alexander in bed with Porchia. The two wrapped in each other's arms and the thin white sheets doing little to conceal what had transpired. The sheets clung to their sweaty bodies.

Cashmere felt the rhythm in her heart shift. Her breath fractured for a beat. Her hand pressed onto her stomach; this feeling, a sourness gnawed at her. Something in her hurt more than she cared to give voice to. Her eyes blinked in rapid succession, fighting back whatever wanted to be unleashed, her breath quivered as she shook herself free from any thoughts. All were distractions. After a breath she moved on.

Keep going, she said in her head. *Keep going*, she whispered as images of Porchia and Alexander intertwined hit her again and again and again. She sought out numbness.

One thing was certain for Cashmere was that she was making the right decision. Up until now all her petty scheming had been child's play and for the cameras. Tonight, wouldn't be any different. She was sure there was a camera tucked in a corner somewhere zooming in just as she came into the aftermath of Alexander and Porchia. There would be nothing after tomorrow. She knew there would be no ticket to Paradise Island for her from Alexander since tonight she'd successfully end any future participation in the show. And she was glad for it.

Her plan was simple. It always had been. When the time came for her own defeat, she would take someone down with her. In her mind, from the moment she joined the show, it had to be Porchia. Porchia represented a problem in Cashmere's mind; one she could never admit to, a fact she might only just be discovering now as she poured the blue food coloring into Porchia's shampoo and conditioner.

Cashmere remembered her conversation with Alexander earlier in the day during the group date. The interaction was mired with the usual and yet something shifted. Cashmere forced the memory from her mind as she emptied the blue ink into Porchia's toothpaste. Cashmere was afforded the added bonus of direct access to the dress Porchia intended to wear for the double elimination ceremony the next day. Porchia was always in a dress, as were most the girls, all except Cashmere against the direction of the producers. Retrieving her weapon of mass fashion destruction, and with little doubt, she went to town on Porchia's dress of choice.

For Cashmere's final trick she swapped out Porchia's expensive skin sensitive makeup for a knockoff fashioned in a similar container. Everything was in place and she allowed herself a moment to smile. It was about to be over finally. She could resume her job as band babysitter, her unrequited love for Dallas, and pretend she'd never met Alexander Ernest Roth. Her life could find it's routine again.

As she crept across the room, she noted the two were no longer in each other's arms and Alexander had rolled away to his side. She would have kept on across the room, exited it, returned to her bedroom, laid down and had a dreamless night but something about the sight stopped her walk across the room. She wanted to ignore the feeling, the interest that seemed to seep into her being.

She had just made it to the door, her hand poised on the handle, when she looked behind her and watched the slow lift and fall of his body. It latched onto her. She drew nearer. She watched Alexander sleep and knew this would likely be it. Ever so gently she bent down and placed a kiss on his cheek, her lips lingered, she watched him from this closer angle, smelling him and letting the sensory both overload and confuse her. He stirred and she backed away.

Just as she made it to the door and began to close it as soft as possible she thought she'd heard him mumble "Cass". She let the idea consume her for a moment before shutting down. Because today was her last day and she knew it.

And so did Ernie.

As Cashmere's hand lingered on the door handle, having not closed the door another memory took hold of her. As if to beg the question *Are you sure you want to do this? Are you really giving up now...?*

"You hate it when I call you Ernie, don't you?" Cashmere asked as she sat across from Alexander. They were the only ones left in the small office.

He shrugged, "I've noticed you tend to call me that when you're pissed off with me."

"That is an interesting observation," Cashmere mused.

Alexander peeked up, away from the thick packet of documents he held in his hands. He smiled at her and said nothing else.

An exhaustive release of ass air brought Cashmere back to reality. She considered looking back in the room but another truth flashed in front of her mind's eye and she closed the door.

She didn't look back.

Chapter 2

Alexander

"Big decision tonight." Rick Hudson, the Paradise Island host, remarked as he pulled up the pants of his white khakis before taking the seat opposite the man of the hour. Alexander noted that Rick looked more orange than usual. The host was infamous for his trademark tan and porcelain teeth but that seemed overdone today.

Alexander offered a smile to Rick. "It is."

"Ready," someone yelled from the back.

Rick turned away from Alexander and just like that the recap show commenced. The ladies hadn't been brought to the stage yet. Alexander still had a moment alone before things would go south. All night he'd had his regrets. Porchia was a mistake. A necessary mistake but a mistake nonetheless and she'd known, she felt that there wasn't much between the two of them. He was confused enough as is.

What was that? He wondered again and again about that almost moment with Cashmere. He'd dreamt of her. Thought he'd heard her. Felt her. The more his mind stirred with her, his hands ached for that slight touch, the harder it was to shake.

"Shall we do a run-down of things so far?" Rick suggested, before an answer could be provided, "Do we care about a recap of the lads that's bit the dust so far? No, yes? Why not? You know I think it'd be good to give a nod to sweet daring Xandra." Rick tossed a smile to Alexander, "She was the female version of our bachelor after all. Had a mean overbite that one, but that long dark hair, oh a raven she was!

"And Sophie!" Rick raved, throwing his arms in the air.

"Amber," said Katie, the girl that handled Rick's makeup detail. There was a whole pit crew. She was one of many that often tackled the job. "Why do you always call her Sophie? It makes no sense."

"Darling, I must've known her as Sophie in my previous life. She looks, walks, talks like a Sophie so she is Sophie personified, but if I must," he huffed.

"Yes you must," Katie answered as she powdered his face. Katie was a quiet beauty Alexander observed. He had to really. The show, in a short amount of time, had made him become more tuned in to women than he ever had before. Even though Katie wasn't a contestant he acknowledged her, mostly because all the girls loved her. Cashmere spoke kindly only of her.

In this competition he'd noticed she seemed open to Katie, not even Emory, Cashmere's friend, could successfully pull the rod that was jamming her circuit. But Katie with her dark crop of blonde hair, sharp nose, and lips that seemed forever chewed upon, was able to break through a wall that refused to be cracked.

"And you're next," Katie smiled to Alexander, "I think Cass will be doing it."

Alexander's face paled at the thought but other parts of his body deceived him in its reaction. Katie appeared to take notice, "Oh calm down. Ash isn't that bad."

Alexander blinked and his head calmed, she hadn't said Cass. *Ash, not* Cass, he repeated for only his ears. He'd heard what he wanted to hear. He should've known that he'd misheard her after all not many people knew that fact about Cashmere and her nickname. He was sure not even Katie did. No, that had always been their secret from day one. It was one of the many secrets they'd shared and kept between the two of them. As well as the promise. He still didn't know what to make of her request yesterday. Only that he hadn't expected it and knew he wouldn't say no to her even though a part of him had grown curious. There was something more. He was sure of it. The tent in his pants was sure of it.

"Grandma James. Grandma James. Grandma James," Alexander repeated to himself.

"Whatever are you doing darling?" Rick waved from behind the latest brush of makeup Katie attempted to apply.

"Just thinking everything through," Alexander replied.

Rick narrowed his eyes, "Thinking about that hot romp I bet. Want to give a gal a quick rundown of that before the cameras start rolling."

Alexander hadn't, not really. He was still mourning that transgression but Porchia was convinced she could change his mind and he was in a state after Cashmere's declaration. His disadvantage was Porchia's advantage and she saw to it. He couldn't blame her for it though, despite wanting to, he couldn't even blame Cashmere, not even Raquel. In his mind, try as he might, the reason he was on this show to begin with was due to his own weakness and last night it showed itself in his inability to handle Cashmere's request. His intent to prove a point to his ex-fiancé, Raquel, was backfiring with each day that passed.

The other stylist, Ash, came out just then. He rushed directly to Alexander, "So sorry I'm late. Had a fashion emergency with Fox and she would NOT rest until I fixed it. You ready for me," he asked Alexander, who simply nodded.

"Get ready quick sweetie, we're on in five. You ready for an explosive double elimination?" Rick asked Alexander.

"I am."

He wasn't.

He wasn't ready to let Cashmere go, but they both knew he should.

The girls weren't escorted out yet. Rick was going to wing it. The last two eliminations he'd incorporated something different. Neither Alexander, nor the set, expected anything different this time. The real catch would be if they'd keep it. Or if it found itself on the cutting room floor.

The sun was bright, but the lighting was extra blinding at the request of Rick. Rick had that old Hollywood look about him. Strong jawline, sharp eyes and nose- he had a vain Bob Barker look about him that no one dared mention. Any sort of comparison drew the same comment, "I don't have as many wrinkles. I'm more of a refined Ryan Reynolds, don't you think?"

The correct answer was no answer at all as Alexander grew to realize. For a slight moment his mind wondered if this observation was the source of Rick's feud with the popular host Trevor Colton. As he looked over to Rick whose lips were poised to move. Alexander leaned forward in anticipation of the distraction from other thoughts.

"Xandra Martin, former beauty queen and first to be let go. The willowy lovely seemed too heart-broken, after all her parting words were, "It's weird our names are so close, like we might be thought to be siblings.' I don't believe our Alexander regrets that one. Dodge a bullet huh?" Rick said.

Alexander smiled. There was always the chance a camera was positioned in his direction. Even though Rick didn't turn to him as he posed his questions, there was always the notion you were watched. Rick gave his all to the camera even as he directed questions whichever way they clung to. They landed was all that mattered and that his face was immaculate in the delivery.

"Amber Thomas, Assistant Paralegal from Philadelphia, may have had the smarts and beauty to match. Who could forget those sky blue eyes, it felt like we were all staring into infinity. Wouldn't you agree Andrew?"

Alexander smiled through this too. Along with aging gracefully, Hudson, as Alexander might have referred to him now due to the transgression, hadn't been the best with names.

"ALEXANDER," one of the producers yelled. Alexander was sure it had been Jazmine that yelled but with the blinding light he was unable to confirm. The only thing he was able to do with absolute certainty was smile through this circus he'd gotten himself into.

Rick waved a finger in the air and there were a few muffled sighs but no one objected. Not even Jazmine. Alexander smiled through it all as his mind wandered onto Cashmere again. He'd caught snatches of her throughout the day without her being aware. The first time was as he snuck out from Porchia's room. It was her silhouette he noticed first, the morning just starting as she stared out the window from the main hall. It was her morning tea.

"...Amber Thomas, Assistant Paralegal from Philadelphia..."

Alexander had known it was her from her profile alone. There was the risk she might have caught him in his daze. He still couldn't explain what happened and at what moment it changed. Except that it had and he was struggling to maintain his word.

"...those magnificent blue eyes! It was as if we all were staring at the endlessness of the ocean. But that personality could have used a bit of work. Doorknobs have more spunk, am I right Alexander?"

Then there was the view of Cashmere as she walked the beach in the early afternoon. At the time Alexander stood near the window on the second floor swarmed by Heather, Hannah, and Hailey. Everyone regarded them as "The Barbies" as they were all blonde and bubbly. There was Princess Barbie, Western Barbie, and Girl Next Door Barbie and depending on the day they interchanged the role. Yet all were engineers, a fact the producers played around with mentioning early on. Alexander wasn't sure how they landed on it.

"But today is no ordinary day. We've lost a few already and our Alexander will not only be eliminating one additional lady today, but two contestants will get the cut. Let's bring out the ladies shall we?" Rick said.

Usually this portion of the day was reserved for Rick's dry run. Him gathering up what he wanted to say for the actual eliminations that evening but today was different. Today the ladies came out all at once. Rick gave his commentary as each appeared; his imposed nicknames that made Alexander sometimes wonder if there was a special place all the hate mail was funneled to. If Alexander was correct with his timing the Xandra elimination was airing tonight.

Rick rattled off the names from Francesca 'Sly Fox' to the Barbies to the Old Soul there was no shortage of descriptions. It was here Alexander had to work hard to not flex the muscle in his jaw, to keep his gaze steady and untrained even as he pretended to not see Cashmere in her yellow sundress, unusual for her, that accentuated her curvy body. Alexander always laughed when he remembered their informal introduction backstage. She was the fill in girl for the previous 'curvy' girl that had backed out at the last minute. Cashmere was the replacement. And not known by many was the fact they'd known each other before.

"If you're looking for the sort of plus sized girls with jelly coming out the sides for you to stick your knife in, I'm not the one," she'd said at the time. Alexander fought with all the willpower he could muster to not laugh because the comment had history, one that Cashmere would not let him live down.

"Porchia," Rick exclaimed, "You look quite stunning today and if I'm not mistaken there's a fairly warm glow about you today. Are we feeling cocky?"

Per usual Rick was making stuff up on the fly based on details that had already been shared with him. He hadn't looked up to address each of the girl's presence because if he had, he would've noticed Porchia's absence; the slight bewilderment of some, the darts thrown to one, and the unmistakable smirk on one Cashmere Watson.

Alexander noticed it all. He inwardly grimaced at the double meaning of Rick's statement. However, the smile still on Alexander's lips, he hadn't spoken yet and he wasn't prepared to explain the night he and Porchia had. He couldn't shake the guilt. He didn't bother looking at Cashmere and the way her yellow sundress clung perfectly to the shape of her body. The wavy look of her wet hair pulled back into a single ponytail. It was a quick job because Cashmere wasn't out to impress anyone today. Except the fact that she'd worn a dress, the one detail gave something away in Alexander's eyes.

Alexander remained seated. As the stage hands ran around looking for Porchia, Alexander snuck glances at Cashmere. Her eyes were diverted elsewhere. His cheeks hurt, amused at that smirk on her face. No doubt she wasn't going to go quietly, even if it was by choice.

Who was the real villain he wondered at that moment, at Porchia's absence, and if maybe, was it possible, that Cashmere might've known what happened last night? Things traveled quickly and it was possible the same detail Rick was in the know of had already made its way to the other ladies.

Two stage hands ran into the house. The Barbies huddled around each other. It seemed in the chaos of figuring out where Porchia was that Alexander for the first time clearly established the alliances amongst the contestants and where the stronger cliques resided. For instance, The Barbies were dressed similarly and he didn't doubt that their leader, Porchia, wouldn't be too far off from today's shades of blue. By the second day of the show, the coordinated color of choice was coral.

There were two non-domestic crews one which consisted of Francesca, Tonya, and Khloe; then the other that included Qamar, Millenia, and Haruka. The last group was a hodge-podge of the remaining women who at any given time might've been spotted together or not. They weren't exclusive to one another yet didn't mingle with the others as much with the exception of Ethel, the old soul, Rick had dubbed her, who seemed to flow in and out as she pleased.

A delay had just been called, Rick was requesting a make-up refresh, and Alexander tried to catch Cashmere's eye to give her the signal when Porchia burst out of the house. She strode with her head held high. Several members of the crew tumbled after her. No one said anything. The silence was answer enough. Once onstage Porchia flicked one glance to Cashmere before she settled. The Barbies came to surround Porchia and the other girls said nothing. Even Rick was momentarily stunned; there was a gleam to his eyes that disappeared just as quick.

Cashmere's smirk returned. Alexander recognized the smirk for what it was and stared at Cashmere who mouthed, "Your move."

Chapter 3

Cashmere

Nothing great ever happened in Tré Jolla according to Emory. Cashmere had always considered it a step up from the Midwest. She'd nicknamed it Lil Trey and thought of it as her 'I made it' declaration. It was her come up. She'd survived. She was a survivor.

People from here argued Tré tried too hard, it wanted to be like its big sis San Diego, but Tré didn't have the tata's for it, cojones for some, depending on who you talked to. But Cashmere saw her. Tré loved so hard that people forgot what it was like until it'd been taken away.

"This is the fucking problem with 90's RnB," Emory said as he leaned over the bar and reached to pour his own drink.

Cashmere nodded.

"I fuckin love this song," Emory started, "but damnit if it doesn't make me feel lonely as shit."

"And hor-"

"Don't start chick. You call me out, I'll call you out."

Cashmere took another sip. She felt the warmth of the evening sun as it set behind them and the breeze kicked up by the ocean. All at once she felt the loneliness settle within her and how the atmosphere at this very moment represented all that was wrong in her life.

Emory popped back down on the bar stool beside her as he used the bar fountain gun to add Sprite into the remnants of what was left in his glass. *It was definitely something fruity... pineapple juice? Orange juice?*

"Drink in?"

In Cashmere's head she'd planned to ask "what were you drinking?" but what actually escaped was a confused question.

"You getting cold out here?" Emory asked.

"I think SnapChat teaches people to hate how they look." Cashmere said instead.

"Oh shit, here we go, waxing poetic, you're cut off sugar lips," Emory said as he downed his glass. The bartender came back over.

"That black shirt is clinging to his body like its life depends on it," Cashmere whispered to Emory who spat out the last little bit of his drink.

"I can hear you Cashmere. And you're both cut off. I don't have time to babysit you two tonight."

"Take a good look at it, look at it now, might be the laaast time you'll eva . . .—" Emory was abruptly cut off by the bartender's hand.

"Wow, has your hand always been that huge Carl? It's in HD," Cashmere said leaning over. She adjusted her yellow tube top, but gravity was against her doing two things at once and she went crashing into Emory. The two landed with a clatter of stools and knocked over glasses into sand.

"Caaaarl, help, we've fallen and can't get up," Emory shouted as Cashmere attempted to roll off him. He instead clutched onto her. "Promise me we'll always be best friends Mere-cat."

"Promises promises," Cashmere said. "What happened to hooking me up with a job?"

"Promises promises," Emory echoed as he loosened his hold.

"Hey, do you two want some help?"

Cashmere was slow on the uptake. There'd been a look on Emory's face that she hadn't been quite able to read.

"Ugh, I forgot to avoid drinking with you. Or at least I should've waited," Emory finally said. "Mere-cat, 'member you're still under contract. Just because you're off the show by your own doing," Emory mumbled the last part, "doesn't mean you're officially done-done. The contract for the show lasts 'til December."

Cashmere ignored Emory and reached for the offered hand. Part of her saw Alexander or thought she had, but it was just a beautiful brunette who could have easily been on the show. Was the girl part of the show? Cashmere hadn't made many enemies during her brief stint, but hadn't bothered to get to know everyone either.

"Heather?" Cashmere asked as she took the hand and envisioned the weight of her snapping the slender girl in two. She retracted her hand and pushed herself up. Emory, no help at all, followed suit. They dusted the sand off as much as they could but it was futile.

"No, but I'm a fan of 'Paradise Island'. It's totally scripted right?"

Cashmere opened her mouth to sigh. She reached to her side and gently guided Emory forward as a wave of nausea hit. She'd overdone it.

"My client isn't at liberty to disclose information," Emory said. Cashmere had to hold back the laugh that bubbled in her throat. The extra deep bass that Emory invoked in that short sentence was enough to send her overboard but the over salivation in her mouth was a reminder not to.

The girl, not-Heather, said something else but Cashmere hadn't stuck around. She walked with legs that felt like Jell-o into the inside of the bar. Despite the bright evening sun outside, it was nearly pitch black inside. Most people settled on enjoying the weather in Tré even if evening brought a cooler breeze.

Cashmere hadn't made it to the bathroom before she collapsed into a booth. Her mission temporarily suspended as she observed the booth. Its burgundy pleather upholstery was slightly ripped and revealed tan padding.

As she poked her finger into the cushion she thought, somehow, she might feel it. That the wound in the pleather was like her own: visible on the surface, if anyone cared to look. As it was, she felt nothing and yet something festered. She pressed further into the cushion until a ding from her phone pulled her attention. A notification, and with it, a possibility.

Alexander.

She was annoyed with herself one moment by the thoughts and emotions that came. This love sickness over a guy who hadn't cared enough about her in the past and didn't now. Still, she retrieved the phone from God's pouch, her breasts expertly kept the outline of her device hidden, and frowned.

Emory.

No sooner had the text arrived did her friend come into the restaurant. Emory plopped down opposite her.

"You have a terrible memory when drunk," Emory started.

Cashmere observed, in the brief pause, there was more behind his words. It was true, she knew, she hadn't argued but there was something just beneath the surface that alcohol couldn't be bothered to conceal.

"I have to get back to the set. Still need to do a final sign off for tonight's show and see what was kept from your..." Emory stopped. Cashmere raised a brow and smiled.

"What's left to do, Em?" Cashmere asked.

"There's a twist coming up, requested by one of the execs that you might need to be involved in. My guess it's a live interview based on the swipe voting."

Cashmere shrugged. "You mean the popularity contest? I was always near the end of that. Xandra did better."

Emory raised an eyebrow. "So maybe you aren't as drunk as I thought."

"Maybe. What else?" Cashmere felt her stomach grumble it's need for release. The volcanic tumble of alcohol and stomach acid at odds with the other. Without a word she abandoned the booth and walked off. Her focus was clear. The contents of the evening were ready to escape. By the time Cashmere returned to the booth there were two glasses of water for her, a third in route just as she sat down. It was at this moment she appreciated the lack of lighting. A nap sounded good.

"I wrote down the few things coming up. And texted you. And left you a voicemail."

"Overkill, much?"

Again Emory looked at Cashmere with a look she felt hid something more. "The charity auction is tomorrow night or maybe the next day. There'll be a crew and when I say crew like one person with a phone catching shots of you for extras."

"Creative cutting you mean? This is why-" Cashmere started to respond before Emory gave another look, a 'we've been through this before' look.

Cashmere thought better than to push it. Emory looked down at his watch. She knew he was pushing his luck being out this long. After all, at the start of this show he'd reminded Cashmere he'd basically be living on the "Paradise Island" property for the entirety of filming due to the aggressive timeline. He practically woke and breathed nothing but the show from day in and day out, determined it'd be successful, producing original content around the clock to get the episodes out on time. So much online content. So little time. It was a huge undertaking.

"Don't forget I still have that tape," Emory said. Cashmere hadn't deflated this time. No, this time, she was reminded there was a ruthless side of Emory that lurked just below the surface. She was sure he was on some spectrum. Was tri-polar a thing? Or was that called normal? She'd called him bi-polar once before while they lounged on their fancy white furniture and he'd only flicked a popcorn kernel her way. He'd been in a good mood that day.

"You won't let me forget," Cashmere answered. "Go. I know you need to get back."

Emory hesitated. "You're not driving back. I'm waiting for Dylan."

Cashmere rolled her eyes in frustration and very loudly sighed how thrilled she was by the news. "Emmmm, why? I already have a gig with them tomorrow. I didn't need to see them sooner than that."

"Chill. It's just Dylan. You can sober up safely with him. And-" Emory looked down to his phone. It was flashing with an insistence or maybe it was just the intense look Emory had, Cashmere wasn't sure. Feeling better now that her stomach had been emptied, she opted for something light, something amusing.

"How's Smurfette?"

Emory snorted. "You're going to hell for that."

Cashmere shrugged, pleased with herself. "She had it coming."

Emory gave Cashmere a long look, and it appeared a thought flickered across, his eyes did something once again she noted, but again Emory held on to his secrets. "And don't forget about the auction. We can throw up a stock photo of you for the live swipe event if that's their intent, but for the auction we need you there."

"Gig tomorrow," she said to remind him.

"Priorities," Emory said.

"Promises, promises," they said together and gave each other a smile.

"Okay, I'm going to go. Dylan is going to retrieve my slightly drunken, semi-sober, bumble bee."

Cashmere rolled her eyes, "That nickname... let it die a thousand deaths along with its obnoxious creator."

"I don't know if you'd want that," Emory mumbled as he shot out another text and started to put his phone away when another message came across. His eyes focused on his phone screen.

Cashmere stared at her best friend and although he wasn't being the best as of now, she knew at the end of the day he'd never intentionally hurt her. Though she questioned how good her own judgement could be.

Emory was a self-described 'blerd'. With Cashmere he'd always claimed he'd come up with combining the words 'black' and 'nerd' to create the baby of their union. Cashmere never bothered to argue.

She watched Emory as he pushed back his thick black rimmed glasses as the light from the screen illuminated his face. He rubbed the start of a budding beard, his facial hair fit him, but when it came time to meet with his funding backers he was all clean shaven. The baby face was the more lethal Emory look.

"I'm surprised you're still here. Aren't you afraid Dylan will hold you up?"

"Oh I'm leaving. I've already promised him an hour of my time for doing me this favor."

Cashmere shook her head. "How noble."

Emory's phone dinged with a new notification just as he was setting it aside. As he read the message his face morphed into a scowl before a suppressed growl rumbled in his throat. Cashmere considered offering up something fun again, but her mind was short on amusing topics that hadn't revolved around the show.

"Okay, I'm going." Emory stood and looked down at Cashmere. "He should be here soon. Rest up for the auction. I'll have one of the assistants' text you an exact time. Head home and just chill out. Also MAAD Maxi has survived this long without you. I'm sure another gig without you fetching water for them won't kill them."

This was definitely ruthless Emory that was coming through. Something had him frustrated and she didn't want to know. There were some friends who you could offer an ear to, to try to help, Cashmere knew helping Emory might mean the loss of an ear.

"Tell Porchia I said hi," Cashmere yelled as Emory made his way quickly to the door.

Emory's hand was on the door as he stopped and turned to her. Again, his eyes held onto something but his mouth yielded nothing.

"Sure," was all he answered as he left.

Once he was out the door Cashmere shot a quick text to Dylan, lying about having a ride and letting him know he didn't need to tell Emory.

Cashmere sat at the booth and guzzled down the first glass of water, she nursed the second, and thought back to another time.

"So do you prefer Cashmere?" Alexander asked as he took a seat opposite Cashmere in the booth. "On your application you listed-"

"Yes, you can just call me Cashmere." She looked at him, her head tilted. She knew it was just a memory being imposed on her current reality. Alexander really wasn't seated across from her in the booth, but she didn't mind the fantasy. Maybe it was the alcohol. Or maybe it was something she dared not give power to.

Another memory flashed, them seated on the pool's edge on the Paradise Island property. Cashmere was sure there were cameras around, as was Alexander, but it was late. Despite the night chill Cashmere was wearing her swimsuit beneath an oversized shirt with a large brown bear.

"A bee suits you better," Alexander said.

"Careful Rick," Cashmere responded and to her delight Alexander chuckled. Alexander was dressed in light gray pajama pants and a white shirt. The outline of his body was noticeable, nothing concealed from her imagination. He had a cup in his hand that he extended to Cashmere.

"It's cocoa," he said as he nudged it in her direction.

As she reached for the cup, their fingers touched. They looked at one another.

A voice cleared. Cashmere blinked. Carl was standing there with more water and food. She was still in the booth. She was still...

How was it your heart could ache for something that was briefly tasted?

She realized she didn't want to take the time to know. She had a few messages from Emory that she ignored. She sent for an uber instead. She needed to be done for the day.

It needed to be done with her.

• • •

Chapter 4

Alexander

Tonight it was Quinn. The Nubian Dada, as Rick dubbed her, was let go. Ever so graceful, as always, she smiled to everyone as her long ponytail swayed against her backside. She was wearing her traditional African garb. The elegance of the royal purple and peaks of orange was no coincidence. Her elimination came as a shock to no one, not even her. Quinn was only guaranteed she wouldn't be the first. But Quinn already had her next gig lined up so the timing was just right. She'd always said she had no intentions of being the designated black girl.

Cashmere had been an added bonus in that way since she satisfied that too, for as long as she'd been on the show. At least in Alexander's eyes, he hadn't been privy to the selection process.

Quinn bid everyone a farewell and gave an especially long hug to Haruka. And this was definitely Haruka whose alter-ego, Sakura, had so far only made two appearances. Again, Alexander hadn't known what had gone on in the casting process but there was a formula, a checklist that needed to be fulfilled and he was no stranger to this aspect of life.

The hug seemed to go on forever. No one commented on it but Alexander secretly wondered if it had been a last-minute script addition that earned Quinn an extra buck or two on her last check. Would it even make it once the episode aired? Of course, it would. There was a story to be told. Implied. And sold to the growing captive online audience.

The producers had been very good about that. They'd negotiated with everyone at the start- deals made, contracts signed, things were final from jump all except with Cashmere. Cashmere had always been the wild card through no fault of her own. Alexander was still never quite sure what happened to the original plus size figure they'd intended. Maybe a better deal had come up. No one spoke much about her.

At the table read tonight the women were in their usual fare. Some still tended to dress up for this part of the night even though it was called the fourth wall hour and that was when the façade really came down. To Alexander there was never a wall up unless you counted the fortress that surrounded Cashmere. He was still reeling from the phone call when Rick slapped his hand on the table.

"That's boring! You're all boring. I didn't sign up for this just for it to be the last thing I'd ever be known for. Forget the table read, we need to be thinking through what will save this ship before we're all out on a job and hoping to be picked up by some washed up act dance craze type of show. Because people I can write the check now, that's where our bread and butter will be if we don't act fast. Now think, you, girl, stop reading and take some notes."

Rick often confused the contestants with the PA's, interns, and some volunteers looking to get a bit of experience. Tonight was no different as he barked an order to Millenia and she gave a blank stare in return.

"Gawd, if you were on this show you'd be the next cut."

Alexander fought back a laugh because Rick was right on both accounts without having checked out the upcoming script. Until he remembered there'd been a recent change to Millenia's timeline. It appeared either the fans had some sway or someone higher up had deemed a change. Alexander wasn't sure. He'd fallen more into being 'along for the ride' with every passing week.

"We need something sensational and we needed it yesterday. Ideas, people, we need ideas. Maybe we should have a triple elimination..."

Emory shook his head.

"Don't discount it." Rick gave a look and Emory sighed with a wave of his hand. Alexander translated this action as meaning it was on the 'possibility table' but they were moving on.

Emory looked around the room, avoiding direct eye contact with Rick as he said, "We have plenty as is with the tight timeline we're trying to run this on. No, I think the problem is maybe we're not best using what we already have going for us. Like maybe inserting more competitions and having more lover suite deals. Or maybe we could have a live fan chat. I can think of some people that would really like that. Rick you could even do an after-hours show and take calls, discuss theories on the mole, and it'll be a good way of engaging our current audience, we could at least include those in a secured count of viewership."

"Still boring," Rick uttered. Emory shifted the dark frames of his glasses with his middle finger. Not many people caught it but Alexander and most of the crew had. They chuckled while Rick went to the white board to draw one of his infamous sketches that confused people.

"A fan favorite," Heather whispered. Her hair was in curlers and she still had a light application of makeup on because she was brought up in the ways that women never went anywhere without their face on, even if it was to pick up the mail from the end of the driveway. "You could do the chat as well as an upcoming live show to have the audience vote for someone that was previously eliminated be brought back on the show. The fan favorite could be good since there's still the 'mole' that's in the cast."

"No" Porchia stated flatly, "stupid idea. Something else. And who's the mole? I thought that was done away with?"

No one answered Porchia, not even her Barbies, they too were unsure but rather than look like fools they took on a studious observance of the blank notepads before them.

"The contract would need to be altered, no? More time needed for a backpack," Millenia.

"Bring back," Haruka corrected. She hadn't done this on behalf of Millenia, but for everyone else who might not have understood, Alexander observed. "Maybe an in-depth on Alexander," Haruka added, her eyes darted in his direction.

Alexander felt shifted his body under her careful gaze. Was it obvious that his maintenance had fallen slightly below par? His beard fuller but those were in, right?

Was it in his attitude? He shifted to sit a little straighter but he knew in his heart it was for show at this point. Haruka continued to look at Alexander. He could feel the curiosity of her stare as it burned a hole into his brain.

"I vote with Millenia," Haruka said as she turned her focus elsewhere.

"This isn't a vote Ms. Hong Kong," Porchia sneered. "Maybe this session could do with a more restricted *English* speaking audience. There are just too many cooks in the kitchen at this point. However," Porchia paused briefly, "she might have a point. We could do with maybe an in-depth look."

"What about another group date each day? I can come up with things," Hailey bounced as she clapped her hands together excited to have something to offer. It felt as if her only contribution had always been to fill space, no one often sought her opinion, but here had been different. Alexander smiled at the idea.

"That's already taken care of," Jazmine said before Porchia could form a dismissive sentiment, "but we could do with more ideas. You want to jot some down?" Jazmine smiled and Hailey beamed. Finally, her head down she immediately went to work making a list. Heather and Hannah were happy for their friend. They leaned toward Hailey to help, and dropped from the main conversation at hand.

"I can't work under this stress," Rick started to stand, "At this rate I'll cut myself from the competition."

"Are you the mole?" Qamar posed and Rick rolled his eyes. Qamar was a quiet but in your face type. She was beautiful but her bite was sharp. She reserved her words. Though at this very moment her dark reddish-brown hair was pulled into a carefree ponytail that went against her daytime bob.

"Goodnight! Wake me if anyone develops any better ideas. This is a free night right? I'm declaring it free, I'm leaving." Rick left before anyone else could say a word.

Emory lingered.

"There was a poll," he started and Katie shook her head, as did Latavia, "one of the fan sites hosted a campaign for favorite current and past contestants. Cashmere was strong. Which was odd given the Paradise Island site swipes list her at the bottom. We screened a rough cut of the upcoming episode with Porchia earlier today with the secured super fan group and it's expected to do well, in fact it's been the highest one they've rated so far."

"Editing, that's all," Porchia huffed, "that girl was ridiculous and couldn't stick to a plan if her life depended on it. She broke her contract and furthermore it's a waste. What's the point of him having a vote if it's only to bring someone back? Is this show supposed to go on forever? If so, someone needs to inform my agent and we need to talk contract negotiations again because I didn't sign up to be on a live action interweb soap opera forever."

"And yet you did," Haruka said boldly. A few girls chuckled but most held their tongue. "Alexander, what are your thoughts?"

Haruka pointedly asked him though her eyes lingered on Porchia's just a second longer before looking toward his light brown eyes. "This is your doing, your experiment in a way, yes... No, wait, uh project, right? The September Project."

Haruka was always impressive to Alexander. Her uncanny ability to remember things even if it were only mentioned once. He'd only known two other women like that and neither were an active part of his life currently. *But you could change that,* his mind beckoned to him.

Alexander nodded. "Really, this is Emory's baby," and he looked over to Emory who appeared to be in deep thought. "We should probably start the table read at some point right?"

Jazmine shook her head, "Let's take a break for the next couple hours. It'll be a late night but Rick's right something has to change soon and we need to figure it out tonight. The ratings are great but the producers... " Jazmine started but hadn't finished. She got up from the table and immediately pulled Haruka, Millenia and a few other crew members with her into another conference room. Very noticeably she left Porchia with her Barbies, who hadn't seemed to mind. Porchia's eyes landed on Alexander, and before she could make her way to him he walked off in the opposite direction. Once sealed off into another room he took to the phone.

The phone began to ring. Alexander observed the closed doors down the dim corridor and it felt as if the house were asleep. It was a deceptive type of quiet. People stirred. Ideas unwound. Hearts beat in the rhythm of the frenzied night.

The phone rang for a beat longer. Alexander was tempted to let it go. Nerves prickled at his entire being. There was the possibility she wouldn't answer but when the line finally clicked Alexander hesitated before he whispered, "I need to see you."

There was only one other woman who could comfort the unease that conquered Alexander as of late. Coincidentally the same person had been the reason for his doing the show. The person, a woman by the name of Raquel Thames, that also happened to be his former fiancé.

Chapter 5

Two Years Earlier

Alexander was overdressed. At least he felt that he was for a first date. It was the return to the dating scene after a hiatus and furthermore it was a blind date set up by a coworker. *Is this really how it happened?* He thought to himself as he stood on the corner waiting for the pedestrian walking signal. No cars were coming but still Alexander waited even as a woman brushed past, in too much of a rush to be slowed down. She only paused for the length of time it took to assess if she could beat the car a couple blocks down. And then she was gone.

Alexander pressed the signal again and watched as she click-clacked across the street with one hand holding down her chest and another keeping her skirt down. He had to laugh at the preciousness of her fear of flashing someone versus the recklessness of her impatience but he had to admit, she was beautiful. Her hair cascaded down her back in brown and blonde waves. For a moment he wondered if it was possible if she was the blind date he was meeting. She reminded him of a bumble bee. Her dress with its yellow at the bust had a black and white lace and leather skirt.

His eyes followed her path as she walked past a few more doors and entered the bar that he had planned on going to. *Is this really how it happened? Was it this simple? Could it be?* He wondered again because if it did so far it didn't seem like a bad thing. His on and off relationship with Raquel was confusing, but here was an opportunity to get lost in conversation with a total stranger. For a whole world of possibility and not be stunted by each other's history. It was a familiar feeling, the "newness" of a blind date. Far away from his usual hangouts, he knew he could somehow be freer in this setting.

The signal flashed and Alexander stepped into the street with a smile on his face; he hadn't seen the cyclist racing from behind to make a sharp turn. The two collided. Alexander hadn't seen stars when he landed on the pavement, but the backside of the bumble bee.

Cashmere hated these employee functions. She hated that her life was tied to so much work and so little of her projects. There wasn't enough time in the day to get to it all and her comic often got pushed to the back burner because it wasn't the thing paying the bills.

The required, but supposedly optional, employee gathering was also themed. The invitation recommended wearing the company colors so they could be easily spotted. But Cashmere wanted to blend into oblivion, to disappear, to hang out at the bar and toss back a few drinks before she was due to attend a gig for the new assistant job she'd landed. She didn't mind the band assistant work as much as she thought she would, it helped that the music was actually good and the members weren't bad to look at either.

She hated that she was running late and needed to leave early. She hated the worry of how that might appear. She hated that she was even bothered to care. She wanted to find something to not hate.

As Cashmere approached the intersection that would bring her closer to the bar, she noted a guy standing lax in his business suit. One hand was in his pocket and the other hung by his side as he waited, like a good law-abiding citizen, for the signal to cross; she was amused. From behind he wasn't bad to stare at and once she was near him, she intended to take a quick corner eye peek but was instead hit by the scent of his cologne as she approached. It was as though the wind wanted to derail her. It whispered, "Hey smell this" and she did. Her eyes took on a sharper angle at the scent. It was very male. Very poignant. It did things to her that it should. The cologne with his natural scent was a match made in heaven as far as she was concerned. She wanted to lean into his neck and get lost in his scent. She wanted to be swathed in that scent, his arms... his body-

No. She shook the image from her head, noted the traffic, and dashed forward, accidentally brushing him in the process. She hadn't dared look back in apology afraid that his backside would match the front and her attraction would only grow. There was no time for distraction.

Cashmere didn't slow down. Ignoring her curiosity, she made it across the street just as a car whipped past bringing a whoosh of air that threatened to reveal her blue boy shorts. She walked with purpose to the bar and only paused for a moment, suddenly wondering if maybe he- *No.*

She stepped through the door and the happy hour crowd was already in full swing. She immediately spotted her team and she could tell the table enthusiasm was missing. She could already picture the unbearable forced conversation about the weather, kids, and other teams or coworkers' woes. These things always had a way of coming into play and Cashmere was just never interested. Quickly she went to the bar and took a seat, planning on feigning ignorance if someone spotted her in the designated yellow and black work colors.

"Don't bother trying to call him over," a woman beside her said.

"Oh?"

"Bit busy here tonight apparently."

Cashmere noted the bartender seemed to be comfortable toward the end of the bar where a group of suits were gathered. He was ensuring a successful tip night. She couldn't blame him. If she saw her, she'd probably think 'Minimum wage scrum worker wearing her Sunday best and will tip with change, the kind that rattles.'

"Stare a little harder for us both and maybe we might even get acknowledged," the woman beside Cashmere commented. It was then that Cashmere noted how beautiful the woman was. She was dressed in a simple black dress, wine colored peep toe pumps, a simple ruby pendant graced her neck and nothing else. The woman appeared to be Hispanic, her hair was a severe cut bob that grazed her shoulders, no layers, just straight black sleek.

"You could always flash him and do us both a favor," Cashmere said. She stood up on her bar stool and leaned over the bar, "Woo hoo, hey buddy!" She waved her arms and the bartender flashed her a smile.

"That's more than I got," the woman said, visibly impressed. She looked at her bare wrist. "Forgot I left my watch," she said to Cashmere. The woman slipped her hand into her small ruby colored clutch and retrieved her phone. Upon looking down at the phone she sighed. "This is odd. He must not be coming," she said matter-of-factly.

"Date?" Cashmere asked, having recognized the tell-tale signs. "Stood up possibly? What time was he supposed to be here?"

"We were to meet at 5:30," the woman said with another sigh and looked down to the phone again, distracting herself with checking her inbox and contacts. "Bart didn't text to cancel either."

"Is that your date's name?" Cashmere asked. A smile warmed her face as she noticed the bartender finally making his way toward them when a group of frat boy types intercepted him with their shot orders. She was getting more irritated by the second. She considered just joining her group or awkwardly standing with a lame excuse of why she couldn't stay long. It was part true but she had time before the gig, as it wasn't until 9 that night.

"No, a mutual friend of ours. It was supposed to be a surprise."

"Oh," Cashmere started, "So Bart arranged for a surprise for a friend. What's the surprise?"

The woman laughed. "Me," she said, extending her hand. "Raquel Thames."

"Cashmere Watson," Cashmere said shaking her hand. "By the way, I'm not sure if your phone is fast but it's only 5:20 now."

Raquel shook her head and her hair gracefully glided, Cashmere's eyes glittered with its simple elegance, her own unruly hair tended to be mostly a pain and thus it often ended up in a bun. "My fiancé is a timely man. You tell him to be somewhere at 5 and he arrives at 3 to ensure he's on time and if you need help that he's able to do, he does without your having to ask."

"Oh," Cashmere said again. She really needed that drink. She hadn't wanted to appear rude but she really still needed to make time to mingle; it felt as though she was on the edge of striking up a full-blown conversation with Raquel. As enraptured as she was to learn her hair secrets she didn't have the time to entertain it.

"Our friend Bart was to set him up on a blind date except I'm the blind date. We've been separated really, my fault mostly and I'm ready to admit that I was wrong."

"Why not just be direct?"

Raquel laughed. It was throaty and robust, the air around them trembled with the heaviness, and there was a sadness to it. Maybe Raquel wasn't that type of woman. Cashmere realized she'd answered her own question in that moment.

"My fiancé was trying to prove something as was I at the time. It seems we always are. Now I realize I have something else to prove, that I know how to have fun. I can be creative."

Cashmere mouthed formed an 'o' but she didn't give it volume. She searched for words when really all she wanted to say is 'gin and tonic, no ice'. "Maybe try calling your friend Bart."

"No," she said shaking her head. "This was a bad idea."

"Or maybe a good one," Cashmere said, the answer struck her just as the bartender headed their way again and was stopped. She sighed and turned her attention to Raquel, "Isn't the fact that he's not showing up an indication that he's not interested in the blind date?"

"No," Raquel said, shaking her head. "It's an indication that either something has happened or Bart is delayed in his cancellation. I hope it's the latter as Bart has a tendency for late updates." She gathered her clutch just as the bartender arrived.

His dark hair wet with sweat just as a female bartender came from the kitchen, starting her shift from what Cashmere could tell.

"Those guys giving you a hard time again Vinny?" the female bartender asked, referring to the frat boys.

"Nann, they were just telling me about some freak accident right out here with a cyclist. Told you have to be careful with them just as much as cars."

"Oh, I hope it wasn't anything too serious," the female bartender said as she grabbed a couple glasses for water beneath the bar.

Vinny shrugged. "Sorry ladies, crazy tonight with all these work groups. First drink on me, huh? Nila, can you take care of them? Frank and the guys only let me go to tend to the 'beauties' at the end," Vinny smiled at Cashmere and Raquel, "I think they'd offer to buy you both a drink for your trouble but were afraid of being told off."

Cashmere nodded. She knew how she could sometimes come off and Raquel had the same 'no bullshit' type persona about her as well. Cashmere noticed Raquel had grown quiet. Raquel stood, blinking, and then she reached for her clutch, retrieving a twenty. "Her next drink will be on me. It was a pleasure meeting you." Raquel left without waiting for a goodbye. She went directly to the frat boys. Cashmere shrugged.

"Lucky girl tonight," Nila said.

"Must be," Cashmere said just as a pair of hands landed on her shoulder causing her to jump from shock.

"Hey everybody Mere-Cat is here!"

Cashmere rolled her eyes. She wasn't so lucky after all.

Chapter 6

Alexander

Raquel Thames had had it all. A six figure gig at one of the best firms in the city. The same firm Alexander had briefly worked at before leaving to pursue a dream. The same firm he eventually went back to. But Raquel had always had a strength, when people said her name there was never a short of praise. As her handsome fiancé, Alexander hadn't minded being seen as the lucky one and Raquel's arm candy. The type of arm candy whom had the power to derail any woman, or man, that was unfortunate (or maybe fortunately) able to cross the power couple's path.

She'd given it all up. She left the firm to pursue working at a non-profit. She had to, really, in order to balance out her more morbid ways, which also meant pushing back on Alexander's insistence to wed. It had been Raquel that knew he wasn't ready. It was Raquel that suggested a break. It was Raquel that suggested they be open for a while.

Raquel, as Alexander had always known, wasn't your typical woman. She had no interest in possessing things or people, she'd found the whole notion ridiculous. Even the concept of marriage was plagued with silliness that she had to remember not to laugh whenever someone talked about their ceremony.

It wasn't that Raquel was blind to true love and the idea of soul mates. It wasn't even that she hadn't believed in these things. It was the level in which people took things to prove a point. Alexander had been no different. Looking back on it now Alexander admitted they were both guilty of it.

"These visits are going to cost you," Raquel said as she took a seat on the bench near the pond. She faced it as Alexander crept from beneath the shadows to join her. "There are rumors already and if you were followed by one of those drones, well I'm sure this piece won't be found on the cutting room floor."

Alexander turned to Raquel. Her hair seemed darker but her asymmetrical bob was still firmly in place and all business. Her eyes were green today. Raquel wore colored prescription contacts, while her natural hazel eyes were a gem in and of themselves she was not satisfied by it. She had a preference toward blue and gray. She'd once told Alexander she believed that her eyes had intended to be the color of the sky but there'd been so much darkness that the lighter hues rescinded into the hazel. That's why sometimes you caught flecks of the blue if the light shone just right.

It was this whimsical nature of Raquel that had initially drawn Alexander, her strong Hondurian background was equally appealing but what had always sold him was the unique head on the mysterious beauty.

"You never stay gone long. I'm starting to think I should maybe date myself to see what the hype is about," Raquel said.

"I really don't want to do this anymore."

Raquel raised her perfectly plucked brow, "If I knew all it would take for you to give up this silly notion of marriage..." she started and sighed. She peeked at him but Alexander hadn't cracked a smile. She let the quiet settle in for a moment before Alexander shifted and she pounced. "What are you doing? Giving up?"

Alexander shook his head, not in response, but in exasperation. His hands pulled at his hair as puffs of air escaped his mouth. He bit back on his bottom lip to restrain the scream that tried to escape.

"You're going mad over there," Raquel said.

Alexander was silent. He took several long drawn breaths before he mustered a decent response to a question that plagued him, "What kind of woman encourages her fiancé to cheat?"

He'd asked this before. He'd asked before it in a variety of flavors. He often asked it jokingly, so the response was never a serious one. But tonight there was no funny bone to be tickled.

"I'm not for everyone," Raquel answered in her non-answer joking fashion but Alexander pressed. He pressed through the silence. He stood from the bench as Raquel remained seated. The night was about to end. The meeting was soon to be over. Alexander started to walk away when Raquel chimed-

"The type of woman who knows what commitment means. The type of woman who has seen the *value* of marriage. The type of woman who recognizes her spirit animal as well as yours."

That was another one of Raquel theories. She had several of them when it came to love. Alexander always enjoyed her anecdotes but tonight with all the confusion he could not stand in the storm of them. Nor her.

He walked away without a goodbye.

"You're back!" Kate said.

"I'm back," Alexander confirmed as he stepped into the beach house foyer. Alexander used to think it was strange how everyone always called it "Paradise Island" as if the show encompassed the property. It wasn't even an island. It was Tré Jolla still. However, as the time went, almost two weeks in and about a week into airing the web episodes he understood. Being here, he felt isolated. The real world was still there but something about the property was a world in and of itself, and it swallowed people. Emory was the perfect example.

"Did something come up while I was gone?" Alexander silently hoped nothing had. Given how late it was he half expected everyone to have tapped out and agreed to reconvene in the morning. Granted most planning and setup occurred well in advance he figured everyone was likely counting down the days to cancellation. There was a rumor that the ratings had slipped since the premiere and a lot of people suspected that once the episode showing the fiasco stirred by Cashmere aired, there'd be a gradual decrease in viewership. Then again, it often mattered who you were talking to.

"I tried calling you," Kate said as she followed Alexander.

"Oh," he offered as he took a small set of steps down past the living area to head toward the direction of the large kitchen. It was probably one of his favorite places here.

"We need your feedback on all the contestants."

"Don't you always need that?" Alexander joked as he reached into the fridge for the almond milk. He was feeling thirsty for something else but with Kate around he opted to not mistakenly get drunk, call Cashmere, and hope she'd entertain his request to just hold her. At least that's what he wanted to do. He shook the thought from his head. He really didn't need to be thinking of Cashmere after just visiting his *ex*-fiancé.

"They need it tonight," Kate continued as Alexander drank from the half gallon jug and wiped his mouth off on his arm.

Alexander wasn't in the mood for one of Rick's late-night ideas. He shrugged and began making his way to his room. Stripping his shirt and pitching it in on the rail. He felt reckless tonight. He hadn't cared much for order. He hadn't cared much for making sense of anything.

Alexander felt Kate follow him. She tried to urge some sense into Alexander but when he lost his pants on the stairs she must have realized there was no point. Alexander paused and looked back at her.

"Not in the mood," he said.

"But Cashmere," Kate said, averting her eyes away from Alexander in just his briefs.

For a moment Alexander felt bad. Here Kate was, happily married and probably trying to conjure a way to avoid telling her husband about the half-naked encounter with the eligible bachelor. Or maybe Alexander had just had a hand in rewarding the husband with spontaneous sex. What was really going on? Why had his thoughts... He stopped.

"What about her?" Alexander tried for nonchalance as he turned back around to continue up the steps. Kate attempted to keep up.

"Rick wants to spotlight and do an interview with you regarding some of the current and past contestants for a future sound bite. I think they are leaning toward the fan vote to bring someone back. The mole has already leaked the information and there's an official petition now."

"And they say the ratings stink," Alexander smiled a false smile as he got to his bedroom door. "I'm not doing it tonight. Tell Rick we can meet up after breakfast."

"Sooner than that," Kate said. "Rick wants to do a special and live show and all this other stuff. They wanted to run it by you tonight and get a jump start on some of it. Plus, Emory thinks if Cashmere is-"

"Kate," Alexander started, "I know what you're trying to do but I'm going to bed. Rick and everyone else will have to wait. Got it?" Kate nodded. Alexander stepped into his room and closed the door. He went looking in the dark for his phone and immediately saw the ten missed calls from Kate and a few from some producers, including one from Rick. Who knew he could be troubled to use a phone? He must be serious about this latest plan. Alexander made a mental note to wake up earlier than everyone just to get with Rick but right now he just wanted to make one call.

He found her number and stared at it. He wasn't sure what he'd say. How much he ached to see her? How he'd given anything to have her here in this room right now? The fact that he was willing to get dressed again and meet her anywhere, producers be damned. How could he ask such a thing and who would've believed it? They barely fathomed it, yet here

Alexander was staring down the button that would lead him to the voice he craved the most.

But it wasn't enough to just hear Cashmere's voice. He wanted to see her. He would see her. Throwing on whatever he gathered in the dark he made a call to Emory. *First Emory, then Cashmere...*

"I need a favor," he started as Emory answered the phone, "and if you can make this happen I promise to do whatever you want once I'm back."

Chapter 7

Cashmere

It's a new dawn, it's a new day...

"And I'm feeling like I'm going to murder Dallas," Cashmere muttered to herself.

Dallas was running late again. When Cashmere had spoken to him earlier as she rifled through her wardrobe, he'd said he would be back in time to have dinner with the band, well before sound check. An hour later when Cashmere called, he was on his way and would be there in forty-five. It was now ten minutes before the guys were to go on, two hours since she'd heard from Dallas and there was no sign of him. At the rate she was going she'd be fired this time.

She knew she should've stayed gone. If there was one thing the ridiculously scripted Paradise Island had gifted her with it had been an out from band babysitter. Of course, that's not what her official title was. She was the *Creative Assistant.* The 'Creative' part had been added for her benefit but the only creative part about the job was what lie she could fabricate to explain the absence and whereabouts of any member at any given time. It hadn't seemed like a lot but Cashmere had been doing it for two years now to know the gig was riddled with landmines, every word, every step had to be carefully orchestrated and delivered. Then again, that's why she was so good at it.

But her problem had always been one Dallas Jamieson. For most of the two years she'd crushed on MAADD Maxi's handsome drummer. Never once becoming distraught at the women that flung themselves at him. Dallas, in comparison to his twin Dylan, who played guitar and was the male lead vocalist, was solid. Dallas and Dylan were nothing alike and yet people often confused them. Dallas, in Cashmere's eyes, was clearly more defined from the rigorous exercise that came from pounding one 'Special Lady' each night, as he'd named his Pearl drum kit in a moment of jest. He gave it to her hard each night. The band loved their sexual innuendos.

And the band was definitely banking. In her short absence they had lined more gigs than slots they had available. It was the late summer and already they had events planned next. Pretty soon Mike might have to give up the day job.

"Cashmere," Art said, stepping toward her. They were backstage. Her pacing was wearing a groove into the wood. "You forget this is Dallas," he said. "We'll be fine."

"No it's not. He's a selfish arse, that's what," Cashmere huffed. Art shrugged and was just about to offer another antidote when his sister Amy, their female lead vocalist, called him over.

Cashmere had flat ironed her hair and already she was sweating out the work. Her glorious waves were slowly breaking through. She didn't care. Why even bother if he wouldn't notice? She could picture him running from the parking lot, some arm candy holding his hand with a promise of the tour bus and her bubbly giggles as they danced through the night. The image twisted into Cashmere's conscious alongside the image of Alexander's arms wrapped around Porchia. Cashmere's fists flexed of their own accord.

It'd been two days... No, three days since the incident. Three days since both she and Tonya were eliminated. Three days since a very blue Porchia stepped out and stripped down. The anxiety Cashmere felt dissipated quickly as an unavoidable laugh hit her at remembering the last day.

"Babe," Dallas said as he snaked a hand around Cashmere and drew her to his solid body, successfully swallowing her. Cashmere wanted to get lost in this touch. She wanted it to be something that was only hers but she knew there was nothing unique about the embrace because there was no doubt Dallas had likely had another girl wrapped in these same arms multiple times today. Still, she leaned her head back to look up at him, something she would've never done in the past. Being on the show had done something to her, she came back more emboldened. She came back not wanting to waste any more time on anything or anyone that couldn't invest the same into her.

"You're late," she said. She rested her arms over his. "And you lied," she said rubbing a fine circle into his wrist. Cashmere tried not to get enraptured by the gray eyed Dallas. He'd recently shaved she noted, a small cut showed on his jaw, and she began to reach for it before she remembered. She repeated, "You lied, where were you?"

Dallas pulled her closer. A brief look of confusion crossed his face. Cashmere wondered if maybe her actions had thrown him off, if only for a moment. "Anyone ever tell you that you look like a mad Alicia Keys?"

Pushing away from him, crossing her arms and giving Dallas a full stare on, "Yeah a certain arse might've once before."

"You're killing me, Cashmere. You've broken out the British English now. We still have a minute to spare," Dallas smiled his signature sly grin. The type of smile where his eyes matched.

Art, Mike, Amy, and Dylan walked toward the curtain where Cashmere and Dallas stood. The deafening roar hit Cashmere then. She'd been too wrapped up in everything else to absorb the energy the crowd brought. It was going to be a good show.

Dylan, just as tall as his brother, snatched Cashmere and dipped her. "Marry me," he said, planting a kiss on her cheek. His newly grown beard aided in keeping the two distinct, but it tickled Cashmere whenever he pulled the stunt.

"Can't," Cashmere said as he pulled her back up. "Emory might kill me."

At the mention of his name a faint blush crossed Dylan's face. Emory was his forever crush, whether he wanted to admit to it or not. Cashmere was just a runner up prize, she'd always joked. "How's the show going for him?"

Cashmere shrugged and said nothing more as the MC walked out onto the stage to introduce the band.

Dallas began to walk past Cashmere to join the others when he stopped. "Where's Evan?"

"I thought he was dragging you in," Cashmere admitted, "but he did get an important call about fifteen minutes ago. He might still be taking it."

Dallas nodded, accepting the answer. He looked at Cashmere again and stepped closer to her, "Good luck kiss?"

"Since when did you need those?"

"Ever since you came back," Dallas said, inching closer to Cashmere with a devilish grin on his face. The problem with Dallas, Cashmere noted, was that he saw her, but treated her like the little sister he loved to tease. He didn't see her as the young woman with raging hormones and needs that were desperate to be satisfied with his touch.

The stage lights went out. The rest of the band was on the stage strapping on instruments and positioning themselves, but Dallas was still trying to get a trivial kiss. He quickly caught hold of Cashmere by the wrist and spun her closer. Knowing she'd try to dodge him, Dallas's lips came down prepared. Cashmere, recognizing that Dallas knew her every action, didn't attempt to move. It was all very quick, but when their lips touched it was not how either expected. Their eyes closed. Cashmere hands clutched onto Dallas as a sigh escaped her and that was all it took before his tongue sought hers. A hunger pulled them closer leaving no room for doubt. All there was, was in this moment and nothing else existed as time slipped away.

"Dallas," Dylan hissed from the stage. Cashmere and Dallas jumped away from each other. Once apart, Cashmere took several steps further away, whereas Dallas moved several steps forward reluctantly, as if the two were tethered. His eyes were hooded as he took in Cashmere. She forced a breath into her lungs.

"Go," she said, just as Evan came up from behind and stuffed his cell into his jean pocket.

"Rock out with your cock out," Evan said and the sentiment doused whatever flame still lingered between Dallas and Cashmere. Dallas's eyes returned to normal as he shook free of the hold, the one that made him want to find an isolated room to take Cashmere into and finish what they'd unknowingly started. At least that was how she'd interpreted the look.

"You're one notch away from being the pervy uncle Evan," Cashmere said taking another unsteady breath. Cashmere watched as Dallas took a seat and hit his sticks together. Already she was forgotten but it wasn't an odd thing. When it came time to perform the band got lost in the soothing bluesy sounds of Amy's voice as she crooned out a ballad or gave their soul whenever Art did a guitar solo, or discovered anything was possible when Mike made the keyboard sing. What happened earlier was just a momentary slip.

"You going to get that?" Evan asked, pointing to the light flashing from Cashmere's pocket. She wondered for a moment if it might've been a mistake to wear her hand-crafted fairy skirt, but at least she'd sown pockets onto the multi-layered garment.

MAADD Maxi had just begun playing 'An Endless Moment', it was one of Cashmere's favorites from the new album.

"It's probably just Emory calling again to tell me about the latest drama. Now that there is only one vixen on the show they've had to up the stakes." Emory was never home and always working. He was still constantly bouncing ideas off a disinterested Cashmere. Her body only deceiving her with any mention of Alexander.

Alexander Cashmere thought and a sense of guilt flooded her, even though it shouldn't. She knew this. And yet it still hadn't sat right with her. Cashmere stepped away from the stage and took a hair tie from her pocket. As she threw her hair into a haphazard bun she followed the exit signs until she was outside. Cashmere thought she heard a slip in the drum, a slip on the count, but that couldn't have been. Dallas never missed a beat. She continued onward away from the stage.

Once outside Cashmere reached for her phone but it'd stopped ringing. She was in the middle of dialing when the phone began to ring again. She hadn't recognized the number. Typically, Cashmere didn't take phone calls from numbers she couldn't place, but there was always the chance it might be for a more stable gig or an agent desperate to have her. *A girl could dream* Cashmere smiled as she answered, "Hello."

At first there was silence. "Hello," Cashmere repeated. She sensed the presence of someone on the other end and was just about to hang up when the voice spoke only one word.

"Cass."

Her heart stopped for a second at the secret sentiment.

"Ernie," she whispered into the phone. "You're breaking the deal," she smiled despite the fact she'd dropped the 'E' name and they both knew what that was about.

"I know."

"What would the producers think if they knew you were calling one of the contestants you kicked off? Alexander, you know better."

Alexander's laughter bellowed, deep and guttural, Cashmere leaned against the wall afraid she might stumble from the sound alone. Today seemed impossible. How was it possible to have her world disrupted by two men all at once? One that had barely acknowledged her and another that had previously offended her. Speaking of-

"I still haven't told Dallas what you're up to," Cashmere said. "I think he might find the fact that you're doing one of these reality shows hilarious."

"I probably wouldn't hear the end of it," Alexander said. "Fallen back into routine then?"

"Pretty much."

Alexander searched for words. "Is the website still holding up well?"

"Yeah, but I think they'll be reaching out pretty soon regarding the bandwidth. More people are discovering them each day. They have some out-of-state gigs coming up."

"You going?" Alexander edged. Cashmere knew enough to suspect that the question might've been posed casually but it probably hadn't matched his body.

Cashmere sighed and loosened her bun allowing her hair to cascade down her shoulders, "I don't know what I'm doing."

"That makes two of us," Alexander chuckled and then the silence fell with things that begged to be said. Cashmere's line beeped but she didn't take the phone away from her ear to see who was on it. "I'm sorry," Alexander said suddenly. Cashmere hadn't answered. She continued to hold the phone. "I don't think this is about Raquel anymore."

"Yeah," Cashmere offered. "Then what is it? Porchia," Cashmere regretted saying her name the moment it escaped. She hated that she cared. She hated that of all the girls he'd given in to *her*.

"Cashmere," Alexander whispered but he said nothing further for a beat. "I saw Raquel."

"I have to go," Cashmere sighed, blinking, afraid of the emotion at bay. The words had fallen from her lips so easily. She felt at odds in her own skin. She hadn't liked the feeling, didn't know what it was, and furthermore what to do with it. Alexander was a confused bundle of nerves and she determined exactly what was bound to be triggered- anger, lust, sadness, lo...

"I miss you," Alexander said.

Cashmere said nothing. She held the phone as she heard a voice as it yelled in the background. Probably time for another elimination talk.

"Bye Alexander," she said to make peace.

"Bye Cashmere."

Cashmere slid down the brick wall and sunk her head between her knees. Her hair hid her. She stayed outside the remainder of the show. As people came and went, she sat there feeling lost with her emotion. Time elapsed and before she knew it MAADD Maxi was done playing their set and Dallas was stumbling out the back with his lips sealed over some blonde. Cashmere couldn't muster the strength it'd take to feel hurt but as she saw Dallas, in his element, was all it took. She smiled as she stood and slipped back through the door. The tears were there, they welled up in anticipation, but she wouldn't. He wasn't worth it. None of them were.

"Cashmere," Art called out, "A couple of us are heading to a bar a few blocks from here, you interested?"

Cashmere checked her nails, they were awfully chipped, and there was a pint of cookies and crème ice cream that needed tending to. She was just about to give her usual 'no' when a thought struck her. "Who's going?"

Art pointed to a few roadies. "The usual suspects and I think Dylan. Amy and Mike are doing their own thing."

"But Dallas won't be there right?"

Art frowned. Cashmere knew he tended to notice everything but wasn't sure if he'd seen what had happened earlier. He shrugged. "He might but he's probably occupied."

Cashmere nodded. "Okay."

"Okay that's great you guys are going out to indulge in some drinking debauchery and I would rather not partake or okay you're going and would rather like the idea of drunken streaking through the streets?"

Cashmere lifted a brow. "As in okay. I'm coming," she confirmed. She immediately regretted her choice of words. How she regretted buying him the entire "The Office" series boxed set. She rolled her eyes knowing what was next.

Not one to miss an opportunity, Art swung his arm around Cashmere and whispered playfully, "That's what she said."

Chapter 8

Alexander

"This is the part of being a teenager I missed out on," Cashmere said as her and Alexander fumbled around for the light switch.

Alexander had been in such a hurry to not be seen he'd failed to properly pay attention to the utility closet's lighting situation. He smiled in the dark, it hadn't mattered honestly. There weren't any cameras here and they could finally have an honest conversation.

Except now that they were alone. His body was alive with awareness, her arm as it grazed his. The heat of just the two of them alone in the tight space. He moved forward, his front to her back and he felt it. The moment she released and relaxed into him. His arm poised to snake around her-

"Found it," Cashmere said and something clicked.

Light flooded the room and there was... Katie? No, Kate? Ash? Alexander's mind struggled for footing, with a need to make sense of what had just happened and where it'd gone wrong.

He was aware that it was an assistant in his room that fluttered about. Talking as they moved but the words had not hit him. He should know who, which one of them it was, but part of his disorientation had been the dream, the memory, that begged for his immediate return.

He rolled over and pulled the covers over his head.

"Oh no you don't," came the voice that had not belonged to any of his earlier guesses. "I'm not Katie and this will not come light. We've got a full day Alex."

It was as if Jazmine had said the magic word as annoyance plagued him.

"Alexander," he corrected.

Jazmine ignored him and continued making noise as she whipped around the room. Alexander felt the weight of clothes as they landed onto the bed. He finally sat up and watched as Jazmine occasionally talked into an earpiece.

"So, are we going to delay the auction then?" Jazmine stopped in the middle of the room suddenly and the light from the large windows cast into the spot she occupied. "I can talk to her. And I've gotten candid shots... It's in their contract so no... The ratings are fine, but fine isn't enough for them..." Jazmine turned toward Alexander. "Yeah, he'll be down soon. Alarm clock must've been broke... Okay, give me ten and I'll be down." Jazmine retrieved a piece of paper from her back pocket and quickly jotted something down.

"Your ass ought to be fired," Jazmine said as she finished off her note. "You," she pointed to Alexander, "need to get downstairs. No elimination tonight, but we'll still be recording activity to air as part of a special or some montage. Porchia's mother is here . . . We're going to do a live Q&A tonight without revealing anything. Tonight Cashmere and Tonya's elimination is airing, following the episode Rick will give you a special interview."

Alexander paused. His mind wandered... was this part of the deal with Emory? Did this mean Emory was going to do it, even though at the time he'd asked for some time? Alexander's favor didn't seem to be asking much in his eyes. He still hadn't left to do said thing, but for it to be fulfilled he wondered just how much Emory would ask of him?

Then there was the more pressing and immediate question. Was there anything else 'special' planned for the interview that no one hadn't told him yet?

"I'll see you downstairs," Jazmine said as she rushed out the door. It was almost as if she'd heard the question in Alexander's head and couldn't be bothered to answer it.

It was early afternoon and Tré Jolla came fitted in her best wear. The breeze was just right. The sun kissed Alexander's skin as he stepped out onto the deck off the kitchen. Several crew members were in the backyard. A buffet spread started near the deck and wrapped around the natural fence. Alexander had half a mind to follow the path right out of the backyard, how fun would it be if he could walk into the hedge and emerge into another world?

"There's no escaping," Ethel whispered. Alexander internally jumped. Had she read his mind? Ethel, as everyone including Alexander had observed, was her own force. She participated, followed the script, but seemed to do it her way. She was a woman of average height, natural short curly hair, brown eyes, and an eternal smile on her face.

Alexander noticed the direction of that smile was focused on Haruka who was standing near a hedge bush, and as she stared at it Millenia approached her. "You probably know it by now, but she's on the show as the neurodivergent one because of her alter, Sakura."

Alexander nodded, "I suspected it a bit, though I don't think it was intended in cases like hers."

"That's why no one has told Rick," Ethel joked and they both laughed. "Most thought, or still think, it's because she satisfied the Asian checkbox. Just a double bonus for the producers," Ethel shrugged as she sipped her cup of tea.

Alexander wondered if she'd magically produced that or had he just not noticed. It was possible. There seemed to be a lot of things he hadn't been noticing.

"Think the producers are trying to push that there's something between the two?" Ethel said as a camera several feet away recorded Haruka and Millenia from behind. "Rick found out that Jazmine and Haruka were an item, open relationship, and immediately suggested that the show's final episode end with you two being the vanilla in a lesbian polyship."

Alexander snorted. Ethel smiled at him. "So, what you're telling me..." he started.

"Be careful with the suggestions," Ethel winked. "There are a lot of rumors that are buzzing about. Apparently, the mole has started several. I think *our* producers are going to cave."

Alexander turned to look behind them. His eyes surveyed the inside of the kitchen and overhead to ensure they had privacy.

"Do you think the ratings are really terrible?" He asked as more of a test.

Ethel raised her eyebrow but she indulged him. "No. Rumor is that we're quite strong, to the point that Trevor Colton..."

Alexander turned around, curious at the mention of the name that should not be said would trip up anyone as they eavesdropped but nothing stirred.

"...is wanting to do a show. Apparently approached the networks. Some even think he's called Emory a couple times without Rick knowing."

Alexander felt as though he could be the mole at that point. He hadn't expected that amount of information.

"I hear Emory is supposed to be working on Cashmere about some possibilities. But he's holding off until after the auction tomorrow. That is if they don't cancel it."

Alexander's ears perked, "What auction?"

"Another exposure opportunity to expand the audience, not just the target. Some of the ladies that have been eliminated are going to be there."

Alexander was just about to press Ethel for more information when a few things happened all at once.

• • •

Porchia's mother and two different interns walked toward them. One intern already trailed Porchia's mother, who'd been in the garden and made a direct line to Alexander once she'd spotted him on the deck. Alexander had noted her earlier, but she'd been snagged by Millenia, he thought he'd had some time to leave.

The other intern appeared from out of the kitchen. Their focus on Ethel. Alexander hadn't known his name but he noticed there was a subtle shift in Ethel, a glow that had already been there grew a bit brighter as the intern spoke.

"E they're ready to get some stills of you in front by the Lamborghini and in the garden maze now that it's free again."

"Alexander," Porchia's mother, Persia, called out. "Alexander, aren't you just sick of it!"

"Good luck," Ethel said as she took another sip of her tea and followed the intern.

"Alexander!" Persia huffed as she climbed the steps, he'd noticed she was having trouble with her leg and as he started to make a move toward her one look kept him in his place. She hadn't wanted it. "Have you.." she started, "Have you ever been frustrated by the beauties at the cosmetic booth of the mall? Don't you hate it when they target your pet and peddle you off to some other smut…"

Alexander noted Porchia was nowhere in sight. But of course this wasn't Porchia's real mother. She was just an actress who put up a good act as "Hatter" the nickname Rick had betrothed onto her. He claimed it was due to the intricate hat she appeared in on the first day but Alexander suspected beneath the lie there was some truth to this portrayal. That's why Porchia never seemed to be around, at least to Alexander.

"This is going to be a long day," Alexander whispered.

"Do you like smuts?" she asked as she looped her arm into Alexander and led them back into the kitchen.

Hours later Alexander was back in his room for a temporary break. He'd not seen Emory all day. He'd thought about calling Cashmere on more than one occasion, and he tried to get more information regarding the auction. But the only thing he seemed to know was that it scheduled for tomorrow, but no one knew where.

Or if they had they weren't telling him.

"I could just ask her," he said to himself.

"You could," Cashmere answered. The dream, no the memory, came back to him. The part he hadn't liked. The part he wished he hadn't agreed to. "I think, sometimes we forget why we do the things we've done and it's easy to say we won't see it through figuring the cons outweigh the pros. But Alexander," Cashmere put her hand onto his chest, "I can't anymore. I don't want to."

That tiny closet seemed to suffocate them both as nothing was said for what felt like an eternity.

Alexander closed his eyes and found his phone in his pocket. She was no doubt working a gig tonight. He wondered if he should tell her about his talk with Emory? The one he'd had with Raquel...

Before he realized what he was doing, the call went through, and her phone was ringing. There was a light tap at the door.

"Alexander, you there? It's Katie."

Alexander hadn't answered. Instead, he listened to each ring with intent, as if it held some key. And with every ring he wondered if she'd actually answer. Despite the back and forth this had always been the plan. It was why he'd borrowed the phone from an intern.

Another light tap came at the door and just as all hope seemed to be lost she answered.

"Hello."

Alexander forgot how to use words.

"Hello," Cashmere said again. He heard the music in the back. She was definitely working. Or maybe she was out...

"Cass," he said finally, not interested in the next thought and collapsed onto the bed with a smile on his face when she responded "Ernie".

It was small.

But it was something.

Chapter 9

Cashmere

The bar a 'couple blocks away' was actually across town and required a cab. The few roadies were actually a gang of people that straggled in from hitched rides. At the start Cashmere felt brave. Ready to tackle an adventure, prepared to forget and have the next day as a reset. But now she stood outside the bar and watched as people trickled to and fro.

The night was cool, the moon full, and her resolve in despair. She watched the network of people in their social gatherings, concrete friendships, authentic smiles, shared cigarettes, and she clung to the wall with her head leaned against it. She was looking toward the night sky, hoping for an answer, and finding nothing- not even a fading star.

Cashmere sighed. She toyed with the ends of her frail ends of her powder blue, canary yellow, and white fairy skirt. She wore it since it was her favorite creation from the end of Spring shopping she did in Thrift row. This particular skirt was a collection of lace. And the best part- POCKETS! She wore a red cami because she felt daring. Because she felt bold.

Because she intended to be seen.

To complete the outfit Cashmere wore a pair of leg high heeled boots and a short sleeved black & white leather jacket that she'd 'Frankensteined' herself. All in all Cashmere thought she'd had a winner tonight showcasing her curvy frame even if there was the chance someone might look at her ensemble and wonder if she'd gotten into a fight with her closet. But the outfit felt solely like *Cashmere*. And that was something she could not explain, but only express. It was this realization that strengthened her conviction. That it was right to be here. Cashmere had just pushed off the wall when Art found her.

"You're hiding," he said simply. "And that's unfair."

Cashmere tilted her head, curious about the next line that would follow. Art was always good for heavy flirtation and a laugh, mostly both at any given time. "And why is that?"

"Well clearly you have an advantage. Watching all of us from your ivory alley corner and who's getting the honor of scouring you?"

Cashmere brow lifted. She was going to walk into that one. Art eyes danced mischievously as he anticipated her comeback but instead she wrapped an arm around his waist catching him off guard but he leaned in all the same. "I love this scent on you," he started, "Have I told you I'm quite fond of what that show provided?"

Cashmere rolled her eyes, "Have I told you I'm ready to be spoiled with shots on your dime?"

Art laughed and guided them toward the VIP line for re-entry, "I do say, Cashmere Watson, are you giving me the honor to spoil thee?"

She smiled, "I am."

Art leaned into her ear, "And do I get to spoil thee later from the comfort of thine room?"

"You may."

He chuckled, "So we're still on to watch your epic departure on Paradise Island?"

"We are," she said as she nudged him forward, "And I'll treat us to pizza this time."

"Aw, but I so enjoyed the greasy Chinese food."

"Well it didn't agree with either of us after drinking. I'm okay on having a repeat of that and besides," Cashmere stopped suddenly.

"Grease is better for a night of drunken debauchery. As well as sex, lots of sex but not just any kind, I'm talking jungle monkey I'd hate to be beneath this apartment type style fucki-OH, hey now," Art said just as Dallas and his latest arm candy strolled toward him and Cashmere. She instantly stiffened. She was sure Art felt it and she was thankful he hadn't called attention to it.

"It's a reunion," Dallas said. His eyes landed on Cashmere briefly, to Art's arm on Cashmere, and Cashmere's clutched hand at Art's waist. Cashmere was sure her and Art likely appeared cozier than usual.

Dallas's eyes shifted to Art's who seemed to have an odd look about him. Cashmere tried to process the interaction. It just felt off.

Dallas broke the brief quiet, "Gemini this is Cashmere and Art, guys this is Gemini."

"Aw the two-faced sign, right?" Art asked playfully.

Gemini's face scrunched up for a moment, "Oh the zodiac. I get that sometimes. My birthday doesn't actually fall within it. My real name is Ginni but I liked the sound of Gemini so I changed it last year."

Cashmere knew, from history, that if this line of conversation continued it would only grow worse. And the way her mind felt, the internal reaction that took place the moment she spotted Dallas coming by, she knew any conversation would do nothing to ease the conflict that still raged from earlier. Part of her had always been ready to give up the silly fantasy of her and Dallas. But the kiss from earlier had managed to muddy the water once more.

"You mind if we cut," Gemini asked, "Dal said he knew you two."

Cashmere eyes narrowed. Not in a predatory way and not in a snarky way but the fact Gemini had realized that Art was part of the same band as *Dall* made her curious as to where this latest groupie had emerged from. If groupie was even an appropriate title for her.

Art pulled Cashmere closer. "From around here eh Gin?" he asked.

Gemini smiled, "Gemini and no." She offered nothing else. Cashmere noted the Cheshire grin on Art's face.

"How do you know our pal here?" Art asked just as the line shifted and something within Cashmere fell back.

Cashmere hadn't cared. She wasn't eager to see Art embarrass this girl in his own way. To watch Dallas either laugh it off or get offended, it all just depended on whether or not he'd scored already. In the past Cashmere might have hung around to find out that part at least but no more. Before Gemini answered Cashmere interjected-

"I think I forgot something," Cashmere said and released the arm she'd had around Art's waist. As she attempted to get out from under Art's arm he swung her into him, effectively swallowingher in his embrace.

"Forgot what," Art said looking at Cashmere head on. "Or are you trying to forget," he added in a whisper. "I can help with that." His eyes pierced Cashmere and it was unlike the playful Art she'd grown accustomed to. Someone cleared a throat and Cashmere looked away. Art's eyes had held her and it was if he knew she was running. She dipped her head low and for no reason she could explain she wanted to cry. She hated to be out in the open and suddenly overwhelmed. Secretly she blamed mother nature for the random emotional overload. It had nothing to do with Dallas. It had nothing to do with Art. It was- It just-

"Cashmere," Art said and without realizing that they had been moving they were no longer in the line. Art had guided them off to the side. By the time Cashmere realized what was happening she was back against the wall, her head comforted by it as she stared up into the night sky and closed her eyes.

Art was there. She could feel his eyes on her every so often. The night was still alive with activity- conversations from old acquaintances, laughter from flubbed flirtations, and the wanderlust of the lonely. "Cashmere," she heard Art repeat again. But she kept her eyes closed because right now, in the desire to run she wouldn't be allowed to. She both hated and admired Art for what he was trying to do. For what she herself had tried to do time and time again. Not run.

So she drowned. Her tears built and seeped through her closed eyes. She felt the hurt of wanting something and knowing she wouldn't have it no matter how good she was. No matter how much better they'd be. She drowned in recognizing that her love for Dallas, even if he woke up tomorrow to see the error in his ways would never surmount to anything because what value could there be in anything that couldn't be discerned in two years but be recognized the moment someone else wanted her.

It hadn't missed Cashmere's eyes the attentive nature Dallas paid to Art tonight. Sure, the kiss might have shifted something earlier but what really made a difference had been the show. It always came back to the blasted show.

"I can help you forget," Art offered again. She felt his body cover hers like a blanket. He sheltered her, blocking the surrounding lights and sounds. Without opening her eyes she knew that if she opened them she wouldn't see a skyline but Art's brown eyes as they stared down into hers. Art, as flirty as he was, had heart. Unlike Dallas he didn't traffic women in and out as if it were a buffet and he needed to try out a bit of everything. Art, true to his name, practiced restraint and it wasn't for the women's benefit but for his own. Cashmere observed in her two years that when Art loved, he loved hard, which is why she knew his offer to *forget* was not something he would so easily say nor hand out.

You're being judgmental, Cashmere, mentally chastised, sighed. Dallas had every right to his love life. It was time for her to let go.

She allowed a few more tears. Art accepted these tears. First his fingers brushed away each one, then his lips kissed soft pecks where moisture still glistened. Cashmere accepted these kisses and when finally she opened her eyes his were there to meet her. She stared up at him and wandered what was entailed in forgetting. She wanted to ask but before she could Art's lip were on hers. It was a gentle touch. He held his lips there and neither moved. He came away only slightly, "the first part of forgetting," he whispered huskily, "is kissing some random guy."

Cashmere smiled, "You're not random."

"Close enough," he laughed and came away to his full size. Cashmere took Art in then, all 6 foot 3 inches of him. His tall slightly muscular frame, he didn't have as much muscle as Dallas but she had no doubt he could still give the drummer a run for his money. Art had brown eyes and black untamed hair. He preferred the rolled-out-of-bed head look, some days he slept just right and it worked for him but most days he just looked like the lazy dorky kid especially when he wore his thick rimmed glasses which seemed to hide those Greek features- sharp nose and olive skin. Art was handsome but when he wasn't being flirty as per his schtick as lead guitarist he was reserved, quiet- a quality Cashmere had always been interested by.

"Okay," Cashmere said.

"Okay as in you're okay for me to be your random guy or okay that kiss was not that greatest and I need another one to discern if this requirement was met," Art said as he bit his lips. He moved in a little closer, "Because if it's the latter-" he started and Cashmere finished by leaning on her tippy toes to close the distance. At first it was just a slight touch, no different from the simple kiss Art had done only seconds ago. She'd start to started to step away when Art pushed further. His scent hit her, her mouth opened, and Art took full advantage. His tongue eager as the two escaped one world and got lost into each other.

Cashmere's hand found its way to Art's head as she tugged him closer. A groan slipped from him as the gap between them was no longer one at all. And Cashmere became aware of the lightening firing around her body, the reaction his kiss alone drew.

There was a sound. Cashmere thought she'd heard a sound but then she was also sure she could hear Art humming an approval with each caress or tug she made as if he hadn't wanted her to exercise control. Showing her how to forget and for that she smiled.

"Artemis," the voice said. It was flat without emotion but when Cashmere stopped kissing Art and turned to the right she saw Dallas. She could not make out his features due to the moon light casting only his illuminated silhouette but there was something in his stance that seemed off. Cashmere noticed his fist were clenched relaxed but his body still seemed wound. Putting her hand to Art's chest she looked away from Dallas and back to Art whose eyes were glued only to her. He wore such a goofy lopsided grin that Cashmere couldn't help but smile as well.

"I think we can check that one off the list," Cashmere said. She made a gesture, a slight nudge, to move Art away and make more of a gap but he hadn't budged. He only smiled more and bit his lip once more. His eyes seemed darker than before.

"Maybe," Art started, "but a reminder later on wouldn't be so bad either. In fact, making out with random stranger should be inserted in the list multiple times to ensure proper success."

"Well I guess I better get a roster going," Cashmere joked but Art stepped closer. His head dipped down to her ears again.

"Not on my watch, I'm your random guy for the evening," Art said before being ripped away. "Dall," he said, "Smooth move bro."

"Not cool," Dallas said and stalked toward Art. Cashmere's back still flush against the wall. She watched as Dallas' pointed accusingly in Art's direction, "Not cool at all. We had an agreement. You fuckin' promised."

"Had being the operative word. Shit's null as far as I'm concerned," Art said as he side-stepped Dallas and offered his hand to Cashmere but Dallas was there again.

"Art," Dallas started and his eyes flickered to Cashmere. She noted the internal struggle Dallas. The chaos in his eyes, the restraint in his muscles. He appeared to struggle as he chose his next words, "Okay, fine, can we talk about this inside, please?"

"Sure, it still doesn't change anything," Art said as he walked away from Dallas again and offered a hand to Cashmere, "You're confused but believe me when I say don't worry, it'll be okay," Art said to Cashmere who took his hand. The two rounded the corner with Dallas as he followed behind. The VIP line was nonexistent and they easily walked in but before they did Cashmere stopped. Dallas pushed past them, he turned to meet her eyes before shaking his head and continuing on inside.

"What was that about?" she asked but really, she wanted to know *is this about me?*

"Don't worry," Art started. "It'll be okay."

But Art's non answer had been all the answer she needed.

Cashmere sat at the bar and helped herself to several drinks. Fifteen minutes had gone by since she and Art came in making a bee line to it. Two minutes into sitting there Dallas came over wordlessly, he hadn't acknowledged Cashmere but it was clear he was avoiding her. Art said nothing to Dallas but opened a tab at the bar and indicated that whatever the lady wanted he was to get. He also leaned over and said something else to the bartender who only smiled and nodded. Art fist bumped Cashmere in the shoulder and was off to some private corner to talk with Dallas.

A million ideas circled Cashmere's mind as she wondered about the exchange that occurred outside. She wanted answers to cease her unnecessary worry which seemed necessary because if there was an issue that somehow involved her she hadn't wanted it. Nor had she asked for it. It never once occurred to her that maybe there was some agreed upon not mixing business with pleasure and Art was pushing the boundary. She wished she could be part of the conversation to state that. There wasn't anything going on between her and Art despite her body remembering differently.

Then again if there was such a policy she should've known about it by now. It still didn't make sense seeing as two members of the band, Mike and Amy, were in an open relationship with the other. Maybe the agreement was meant from a management perspective and the whole idea of not doing your dirty work the same place you sleep. Cashmere thought there was a saying for it, she was close, and had just taken her fourth shot when she felt a body saddle next to her.

It was female. For a moment she worried if it might be Gemini. Cashmere dared not stare into the eyes of the woman whose night she'd obviously disrupted though if Gemini hadn't had the pleasure of having her world rocked by now Cashmere might've actually done her a favor. As she attempted to wave down the bartender for another shot the woman seated beside her touched Cashmere's thigh, "Allow me."

In seconds the bartender was over and Cashmere's new found friend, that wasn't Gemini, had already made it into her good graces. The woman was a stunning and quite attractive beauty, Cashmere observed the moment she gave in to her curiosity. Short pixie cut hair, oval shaped brown eyes, and an adorable gap that Cashmere couldn't help but stare at.

"I was telling myself before I came over here 'you don't know her', but I couldn't help it, you looked familiar to me and I couldn't explain why but now I know. It's you isn't it? The girl from that internet show- Paradise Island."

This was a first. Cashmere tossed the drink back. This had never happened before but should've been something she knew would happen once the episodes began to air. That even with her brief stint on a reality show that honestly wasn't doing well in the rating, at least from what she'd heard, that there was the possibility she would be recognized and now it'd happen. But something in her memory banks tickled... Was this really the first time? Her eyes narrowed, her mind was working and finally she yielded. It hadn't mattered she decided.

She didn't know what to think. Being a celebrity, even with her own ambitions, was never one of the things that particularly interested Cashmere even though her named begged for recognition. It had *somebody* written all over it why else have a name such as Cashmere Watson? Another memory stuck then, one she was sure of. One that involved Alexander E. Roth. One that she intended to avoid.

"Cashmere Watson," Cashmere smiled extending a hand in which the woman shook all too enthused.

"I knew it was you. A friend of mine has an uber crush on you, she's convinced that if the two of you ever met and I quote 'she'd move from the dud to a stud'. Her words not mine. So, is it true about Alexander?" asked the woman whose name Cashmere still did not know.

There were a lot of things to ask about Alexander. The non-specific question could be answered with a simple yes or no and Cashmere had a 50-50 chance of getting it right, unless, of course it was something she was unsure of to begin with such as if Alexander were packing. The idea of it made Cashmere's cheek flush, she had her ideas but no clear answer which brought the probability of her answer being accurate to a 33% chance.

Without asking, another shot was filled and Cashmere took it back. Her lips moist from the fiery liquid. The bottles on the shelves took on an interesting spectacle with the light beneath each shelf created an effective colorful glow as it illuminated each bottle. Cashmere was momentarily transfixed by it until she remembered the woman and caught the tail end of what she'd been saying.

"I mean if you're already engaged why go on a show? It's just one of the rumors though but it seems like you don't know much about it either. Are you still reeling from the rejection? Is that why you're out now? I keep thinking there might be a twist and OH! I know. So, one more question and I swear I'll stop rattling your head off about my theories. Still trying to figure out the mole one but it looks like they've leaked something new. Are you a contender for the vote back? If so me and Frankie will totally be voting on your behalf! You shouldn't have left so early anyway. Anyone watching can tell that there was something brewing but I guess if the secret fiancé rumor is true maybe she asked for you to leave? Getting too close and all and if Alexander is to 'win' he can't *actually* find love, right?"

Cashmere turned to the woman. Very slowly because everything felt so off kilter that moment and her mind swam with a sea of things from Alexander, the fiancé Raquel, the mole, and the vote back. The vote back was new. Never had there been any mention of it in the contract, none she remembered at least.

From the show's perspective it'd be financial ruin to change up at this stage given all the agreed upon contracts. There'd be a lot of in-fighting if the rules suddenly changed to have some audience participant type voting to bring back a previous contestant. The more drunk Cashmere thought about it, the more ridiculous the notion sounded but the more it became tangible as well. After all this was a leak that the mysterious mole had likely let slipped to get a feel for how successful it might be. News had traveled fast, so fast that Cashmere was shocked she hadn't heard a mention of this from Emory's mouth. This was surely news he would have delivered to her directly knowing the implications and how unlikely she'd be game for any participation of the sort.

"No idea," Cashmere slur said, "What's your name again?"

The woman smiled, "I didn't give it," and with that she slapped a bill on the counter pointed to Cashmere's shot glass and sauntered off. Cashmere eyes followed her long enough to catch the woman turn around again and give a playful wink before being swallowed by the crowd.

"Maybe I should convert," Cashmere mused as her shot glass was emptied just as quickly as it'd been filled. The bartender noted the quickness in which she moved and was preparing to refill her when a hand covered the glass.

"I do think my lady friend has had enough," Art said leaning over Cashmere, "Miss me, darling?"

Cashmere ignored him and pushed his hand away from her glass, "Another please."

"Close my tab," Art said as he took a seat beside Cashmere and scooted her seat closer to him and made it so she now faced him instead of the bar, "I admit I like drunk Cashmere but we have a date and I want to see vixen Cashmere on the big screen tonight but I also want sober Cashmere to provide commentary. What's a gent to do if drunk Cashmere wants to ruin his plans?"

"A gent should have considered his desires in advance."

Art's eyes narrowed and flickered to Cashmere's mouth momentarily before he fixated his eyes on hers once more, "And he has."

It was then that Cashmere felt more than what she should. A feeling more brought back flashes of earlier and guilt at somehow being caught up in something she'd not known existed. Her mind played at the strings of her heart and with it came an additional swell that she was not anxious to confront. Dipping into her boob pocket she pulled out a bill and waved to the bartender, "Another please," she shouted as loud as possible when a hand grasped her wrist.

"Think it's time to call it a night Watson," Dallas said. He wasn't alone. Gemini was at his side and try as Cashmere wanted to not be affected, she was. She wore the defeat and to herself, she demanded, 'remember this pain, remember it'. She pulled her hand away from Dallas and closed her eyes for a moment. There was enough emotion to flood the bar with her tears alone but she wouldn't cry. She took a deep breath and came back up with a smile. She reached for her phone remembering she wanted to call Emory regarding the mole leak, even he had no idea which of the cast it could be. Not many people were in on that aspect of the show but Cashmere always had her theories and she was positive the host Rick Hudson was likely the one.

"I'm going to head out," Cashmere said as she turned on her stool to make her way away from the bar. But Cashmere was not herself, she was drunk Cashmere trying to multitask like normal Cashmere so when she simultaneously went to stand and call Emory her body was not able to compute the multiple demands. *This feels like déjà vu...*

Is this what slow motion felt like? One moment she was erect and the next gravity was calling her down to join the party except Art was there and held onto her in an awkward stance.

"I feel like I should swing you like I do my niece."

"Is your niece prone to vomiting with motion while intoxicated," Cashmere grunted feeling the force of her weight as Art held her and gently began trying to get her upright again.

"Can't say so, but I bet she'll be an adorable drunk someday too."

"You have issues."

"Tell me about it, on our way to my place unless we can go to yours."

"That doesn't seem... Is that a good idea? Cashmere you want us to call Emory? He should be off by now right? And probably needs a break from the show for a bit." Dallas interjected. There was a tension in his body Cashmere observed and tossed it just as quickly.

"I'll manage," she said brushing Dallas off. "Go enjoy your night with Gemini, I'll see you tomorrow and a lot more sober," she smiled hoping he'd leave well enough alone.

"To my place then," Art started, "I've recorded the episode for tonight and nothing like a nice greasy slice of pizza to help reduce the chance of a hangover."

"Recorded? It's on the web," Cashmere said.

"There was a live piece tonight."

Cashmere shrugged, laughed, and finally shook her head. She wanted to just go home but upon getting erect again she noticed the missed calls from Emory and the multiple voicemails which only meant one thing, there might have been some truth to what the woman said earlier. Emory was likely trying to figure out the perfect pitch to rope her back in if she were to get the vote.

Cashmere wasn't interested in the potential of a night filled with Emory going on and on about why she still owed him. Or why she needed to do the show. Or why this would be a good next step. Or the stupid video… She wasn't interested in the why of anything tonight so she turned to Art, "Okay."

"I'm not sure that's a good idea," Dallas said but his eyes were turned to Art. His fist clenched again, "Listen Cash, I'm going to call Emory. Can you give me his number or I'll just go get it from his number one fan."

Cashmere broke out in laughter, "Dylan might not like your sudden interest." And Dallas winked as he walked off.

"Okay," Art repeated, "Okay as in let's go to my place and gorge on pizza or okay I'm done for the night and going home."

Cashmere checked the bar. Gemini was nursing some cocktail but her attention otherwise averted and Dallas must've wandered to the back in search of Dylan. She turned back to Art and a sly smile was on her face, "I think you know which random guy."

They stared at each other for a moment before Art captured Cashmere's hand and tugged her toward the exit. She was sure of her conviction. She was sure of her decision. She was so sure of the moment.

She was sure to forget.

Chapter 10

Alexander

      In the great scheme of planned activities, if said call had a plan, it failed. There'd been initial elation to hear her call him "Ernie" but none of what really mattered had come to surface and now she was gone.

      It hadn't escaped Alexander's ear, the music that pulsated faintly. He knew it was likely that Cashmere was working tonight and still he took the chance.

      "Write. Less jumbled." Millenia had once said to him. Earlier in the day he'd noted she was sitting at the patio with a pen and paper. "For Sakura," she'd told him. He nodded and as he sat at his bedside the words came together.

"Dear Cass,

I'm ill-equipped. It is not a fair excuse but it is just that, an excuse. You have seen my different sides as a coworker, pseudo-boss, and potential lover… I lost my thought.

I'm writing this letter because I've found trouble with words. There are so many choices, even the ones that have yet to be revealed…. I-

I don't know what I'm doing if I'm being honest. I'm trying to write you but even I keep stopping myself. Second guessing.

Wanting to find the right words. I think that's my problem. I want to make sure I hit the mark and if I don't. I don't. I just stop. I'm good at that. So is Raquel. Maybe that's why we've worked for so long. Perfectionist beneath it all.

I shouldn't have mentioned her... But I don't think you mind. I don't think it's about her.

Sometimes I think we're all just repeating the same mistakes. We think we're controlling something but really we're just falling into familiar traps and it feels like home. I think that's what you might've been saying that day, with seeing this through.

We're all competing. And I guess for me I'm competing with myself. The version of me you see... am I just...? Do I really think I get it or am I pretending like everyone else?

Cass-

Sometimes I just wish..."

Alexander's pen paused. He thought about those next words. He saw Cashmere in his mind as he thought them. Just as he wrote the last words a memory flashed before him.

They were in the office and she was hanging a sign when Alexander moaned in agony, "this code is a fucking... it needs to just die."

His monitor went dark. So did every light in the office. Alexander looked over to Cashmere as she stood still in front of the store window. The promotional ad still suspended in her hand.

Alexander looked across the street where it appeared the electric was still on. He considered reaching for his phone when everything suddenly came back to life. Cashmere eyes were on him.

"The universe is always listening," Cashmere said before returning to her task at hand.

As Alexander signed the letter, he wasn't sure if he wanted the wish to be true or not.

The truth was he missed her. Some days he wondered if it'd be easier if they'd just never met. But Alexander knew that wasn't his real wish, his true desire. These hadn't been the words he'd written but for a moment he'd at least given them consideration.

Chapter 11

Cashmere

Cashmere and Art had just arrived at the parking of RipTyed, a bar known for their signature tie-dye drinks. The lot was relatively empty, rows and rows of open spaces except for a small corner near the building of RipTyed were a crowd of tailgaters had gathered. There were several portable grills out and wafts of smoke filling the night air. Any other time the smell of smoked meat might've tempted a sober Cashmere to investigate and charm her way into a few extra charred hot dogs. But the smell tonight only elicited gag noises.

The cab pulled directly alongside Art's jeep. Cashmere half heard the cost. She thought to haggle and in her mind she was through her mumbled protests. Art chuckled and folded a few bills. "Okay time to get out Mere-mere."

"I hate it," Cashmere whined.

"I know you do. Consider it motivation fuel to propel your way out of this lovely cab of wonder and into the magical school bus."

"I don't want to get out," Cashmere said into Art's neck as he tugged her gently to his side. "I'm comfy," she breathed and for a moment Art stilled. In the quiet that followed Cashmere was tempted to look but was afraid what she might see. She moved and so did Art, neither spoke again until they were fully upright outside.

Art was smiled up to the night sky, "Aww the joys of being in the city and all the light pollution not a star in sight. Mere-

mere," Art said as he took hold of Cashmere by the shoulder who wavered at the contact.

"I'm fine."

"Sure you are. I just like being near you Mere-Mere."

"Stop calling me that."

"Sure thing Mere-mere. So straight to my place Mere-mere where both the DVR and television are cranked, willing, and waiting for us to do very scandalous things to it. Along with the pizza delivery guy who'll have a cameo in the porno we're about to film."

"I can't," Cashmere started just as Art opened the door and watched her flop forward into the jeep.

"Cashmere," Art said in a very serious tone, "I-" and he stopped. Again, that feeling from earlier returned but Cashmere didn't turn to see. She just felt the air stir, felt as though something was amiss that even Art could not joke his way through. "Cashmere," Art repeated again and it was a desperate whisper. One moment there was heat behind her, moving in on her, a hesitant press of body on body. A hand gently landed at her waist and then there was a quick dig causing Cashmere to jolt.

"Get in there properly Mere-mere," Art said thrusting her further in.

"That's what he said," Cashmere mumbled into the seat, "smells like ass."

"Maybe if you weren't so adamant on making out with leather instead of an actual human being it wouldn't be so unpleasant."

"Mmm, nope, human's smell like ass too. And garlic. And onion. And feet," she said, the last on a yawn. "I think I might be sick." Art pushed, sending Cashmere and half her body over the console. She grunted her disagreement but made no attempts to move. Movement at that very particular moment seemed precarious.

Art rounded the corner and yelled out to the group. Cashmere didn't make out what they said. She could make out the joyous and an excited Art, one that was willing to please, who had opened the driver door.

"Come on."

Cashmere heard a guy yell to Art, followed by an upbeat pout that was not male-like at all. A sing-song voice that meant to entice Art with more than just her voice. The idea of it, the thought of being left again for some other, more attractive woman lit the alcohol in Cashmere's belly.

"I can't," Art responded back.

"Pleaseeeeee," the sing-song voice came again, this time much closer.

"Can't, got plans," Art said and Cashmere, not looking, felt the dip of the jeep as he stepped one foot in preparing to sit just as the voice came again.

"But we're having-," the voice suddenly stopped, "Oh," and she stopped again. The alcohol was doing a funny thing to Cashmere's mind. One moment she was raging and clamping down on her lip drawing blood but by the next feeling confused by the rage. She knew she could be her psychiatrist at that moment. Look at the origins of her feelings- why the confusion? Why the rage? Was it Art? Or was there something more?

Cashmere's mind fizzled. She'd started to doze off somewhere when the sing-song voice spoke up once more, "Well she looks like she's asleep. You could come over and say hi to the guys, just for a sec. We won't keep you long."

Cashmere's mind woke instantly but she remained still. Her body still slightly hunched over the console. She could feel the heat emanating from Art's hip as he was still half in and half out the car. '*Make your decision*,' the alcohol bellowed in Cashmere's head. She felt the heat of her rage bubbling again and she didn't care to trace it back. She didn't care to put any expectations on Art because he'd be just like the rest. She didn't want it. No one. She didn't need anyone. Just a trip to an outlet tomorrow for the delayed therapy she still needed from the stint on the show. But she couldn't go home just yet, there was the chance of running into Emory if he planned on coming in tonight. Most of his days were spent at the show but if he needed something, she was sure, he'd made the trip back home.

"Just for a second," Art sighed as he stepped back onto the pavement, the jeep shifting from his exit. "Mere-mere, I'm going to roll down the windows so I don't suffocate you too early. Might be good to let you rest a bit just for the sake of motion sickness and all that jazz. You hear me Mere-Mere." Cashmere heard the beeps from the keep in the ignition. The car waking, if only for a tiny moment for Art to roll down the windows. At the whir of the window an idea had formed in Cashmere's mind about what this meant. It came to her so quick, it left not even a fleck of dust, not the slightest inclination to be traced back toward. She didn't care to fetch for it.

Cashmere had withdrawn instead. Something in her felt heavy, a deep seeded desire to cry overwhelmed her. She wanted to scream into the night but she suppressed it. She held back all *because that's what a strong woman would do*, the alcohol whispered to her mind. She was not weak. She would not show them. She didn't hurt.

"Mere-mere," Art said leaning over her. But Cashmere hadn't budged. She kept her breathing steady even through the erratic shift of her fast-paced alcohol infused mind. This wasn't the alcohol talking though, she recognized that, it was the anger, had always been the anger. The alcohol had simply given the anger a platform to stand on. She felt Art's lips press against her hair, they lingered for a second longer than necessary. Despite better judgement Cashmere flinched but if Art noticed he hadn't said anything. "Be right back," he whispered as he took the keys and shut the door.

As he walked away Cashmere heard the woman with the sing-song voice ask, "Is that your girlfriend?" Cashmere detected something more from the question, something seemed territorial and for a moment she wondered if the voice was one she ought to recognize but instead she was distracted. She was distracted by the slight chuckle and the potential answer.

She hadn't heard one.

Cashmere waited about five minutes before she mustered enough strength to get her body vertical. She wasn't sure if this was the best plan but she hadn't wanted to wait for Art to have his fill of women and booze then attempt to drive them back to his place only for him to shamelessly flirt while they watched the sabotage episode of Paradise Island.

Nothing about that scenario sat right in Cashmere's head especially the part where he flirted after having gotten laid. She hated how the guys could do that sometimes even Mike might tease a girl but Amy never seemed to mind. Cashmere envied the cool way Amy handled things; she took everything in stride.

"How can you stand it?" Cashmere asked Amy once as she nodded over to the bar where a woman was attempting to get friendly with Mike. Mike smiled. Cashmere noted the woman had a well-manicured hand over his shoulder, he leaned into the woman's personal space, all he had to do was sneeze and they'd be making out furiously. At least that's how it appeared to Cashmere.

"Oh boy," Amy said her eyes bulging, "She's trying so hard now, look how she's invading and he's trying to be nice but she's not getting an inch."

Cashmere's eyebrows shot to her hairline, "Are we looking at the same thing?" She asked turning to Amy who was dressed beautiful as always and all legs in her black leather skirt with thigh high boots. The band was relaxing having just finished their set and enjoying the main act. Amy's Greek goddess features were already drawing stares. Her long dark hair pulled into a sleek ponytail that only enhanced her sharp brown eyes. It was with those same brown eyes that Amy said to Cashmere, looking dead on, "This is what trust looks like sweetheart."

Just like that Cashmere felt dismissed that night but that hadn't been the point Amy wanted to make. Cashmere knew this and still she felt hurt on multiple levels about the ease in which Amy had handled things when it came to Mike and other women. She eventually declared the two were in an open relationship because it seemed more logical. And to this day, knowing Mike and Amy were fully committed to the other, she still held the same logic.

"Can't trust them," drunk Cashmere uttered.

"They're not all bad" reasonable Cashmere offered.

"No, never again," drunk Cashmere said as she reached for her phone.

"Just need to stay here until Art gets back."

"No," Cashmere said as she fumbled with her phone before dropping it. The battery was low and her attempts at locating a nearby cab company was met by fat-fingered keystroke errors. "Frick it," she said and opened the door. The cool night air hit her immediately. She shivered against it. The music was louder, noticeable, and strange how deaf she'd been to it. Without a doubt she placed Art's bass filled voice as it belted out a few notes into the light polluted night. The smell of the meat still bothered Cashmere however. She made her way away from the music, the food, the people, the everything and hoped that everyone would be too engaged in each other to notice the woman who stumbled out of the parking lot. She thought she heard someone yell "Hey miss!" but she was too tired, too desperate, to bother to turn around.

"Gonna take these runaway bags and show that I'm the
one-
Been standing in front of you, your only son
Yet you don't do well seeing me, seeing you
But darlin' it takes two
So maybe once I'm gone
You'll recognize you've got none..."

● ● ●

Cashmere repeated these lyrics as she walked aimlessly. She wasn't sure how long she'd been gone and felt a few beeps from her phone but no calls. At least she didn't think there'd been any which only meant Emory was texting her like crazy and Art was otherwise engaged in nailing his latest groupie. The perks of being a band babysit- assistant, band assistant. Cashmere had just passed a strip of night clubs that hadn't let out quite yet but there were guys standing about. A few called out to her but she was just steady enough to show her lack of interest. None pursued. A couple blocks further she spotted a 24 hour diner and her eyes lit up.

"Sanctuary!" She yelled to no one in particular. Inspired to take a selfie Cashmere fished her phone from her bra and was surprised to see twenty missed calls. But those could wait. She was sure Emory had grown desperate because she had over 100 text apparently. Knowing Emory he'd enlisted help, probably even had Alexander in on it as well. Her mind paused at the thought of Alexander in nothing but his boxers, sitting up in his bed, and furiously texting messages to her hoping that at any point that one of his texts might be the one she actually responded back to. Cashmere got a sick sort of glee from it. And then she got sick. She stopped between two buildings attempting to get away from watchful eyes as she lost her gut for the third time tonight, "Never again," she said after the world's loudest blech ripped through her core. Her lips glistened from her latest ventures in bad drinking choices.

Cashmere made several wobbly steps back toward the street though part of her was anxious to have somewhere to rest her head, and the wall appeared inviting. But she knew resting her head was a slippery slope to passing out so she staggered back on the sidewalk and made it the short distance to the diner. She stepped in and saw it was severely occupied.

She'd make friends.

The first booth she wandered to sat two girls who obviously were not out for a night of dancing, they looked like students with their text spread out on the table. They looked at Cashmere in unison as she approached.

"I hate to bother you," Cashmere started and fought for steady, reassuring voice and not drunken slurs, "But do you mind if I join you." She added 'please' as an afterthought. The girls looked at her as one of their eyes lit up behind her black frames.

"Sure," the blond offered, "I'm Lisa, this is Meg. You look really familiar to me," Lisa said. Cashmere smiled and offered nothing else. A couple minutes later the staff wandered over and while Cashmere was hungry, she wasn't sure she should risk eating let alone afford it as she couldn't remember carrying her wallet. So, she sipped on water instead and apologized in advance as she placed her head on the table and passed out while the girls worked through their school work.

Cashmere had only closed her eyes for a few seconds it seemed but she woke to flashes and a crowd. She knew how things usually went when it came to her sleeping off a night of bad decisions but waking… She heard women squealing, keys tapping, people shouting "Get your photo with the rogue one", "Cashmere in the house", "Hashtag Cashmere dreamin", "Hashtag ParadiseIslandVixen…"

"We're trending!" Someone yelled from across the diner. And a sharp yelp afterwards as the chime of the diner door shook violently as someone entered.

"Cashmere!" called a voice that she was sure she recognized but had never heard it sound so menacing before. She didn't have to wait long, nor was it hard to find her as Art, face red, spotted her at the corner booth. She noticed then that a note had been tucked under her arm from… Lauren? Mildred? …Marge?

"No worries," it started, "we didn't sabotage your drink while you were out."

She hoped the night wouldn't get any worse but knew from experience to not ever request such a thing because things always did.

Art was silent the entire ride. Getting out of the booth, out of the restaurant, and into his illegally parked red jeep had been a difficult task but at least Cashmere was a bit more sober. She figured Art was drained from the exercise of escorting a D-rated celebrity. The episode had finally aired and the small cult following the reality show had acquired had come out in droves when they realized THE Cashmere was at the tiny diner passed out from a hangover. It was the type of celebrity-ism that would drive anyone mad, or in Art's case to complete and utter silence. It was annoying because Cashmere felt as if she was still owed to be pissed off at him instead but as they made it to his jeep and Art held open the door she saw it in his paled expression. The deep shadows haunting his face and the malice in his tone when he said, "I called you." It was in the infliction, a sadness that made her realize just what might've gone through his mind.

But as Art took his breath once Cashmere was safely inside she watched as he leaned against his jeep and gathered himself. He was fuming. She'd never seen Art anything other than playful and he was fighting to keep calm. His hands ruffled then tugged his dark mane as if he needed to be free of everything. It was during that time that Cashmere took stock. There'd been two missed calls from Alexander, three from Emory, less than a handful from a mixture of the band, including Dallas, but the majority was from Art. He took the cake with over 20 missed calls and it was no wonder as she observed the dashboard, it was nearly five in the morning, she'd been gone hours, passed out in a diner sleeping away her hangover while Art searched the streets not knowing where.

She couldn't hold on to her anger even if he was with a girl for a portion of her absence, no friend deserved that much worry, but she was an adult another part of her brain argued. Looking over to the steering wheel she saw the whites of Art's knuckle as he clasped the steering wheel. She opened her mouth to say something but couldn't find the words without somehow throwing her own jab for his own negligence but how could she be upset how he spent his night, they weren't an item. Again, Cashmere was confused. She was looking for something and was looking for it in all the available outlets. Constantly attaching herself to the possibility of more when an offer was never on the table. She sighed and swallowed the self-hate that followed.

They pulled up outside Art's place. Neither said anything, the horizon was still dark but dawn would come soon.

"I'm sorry," Cashmere said at the same time Art asked, "Should I have Emory pick you up?"

Art faced her, his eyes still burdened by the thoughts that no doubt crossed his mind about her in those hours he couldn't account for. The circles that formed around his eyes made it hard for Cashmere to look at him, she turned back toward the window. "Did Emory say he was home?"

"No, but he told me once I found you, I should bend you over and-"

"Got it," Cashmere interrupted; she had an idea the type of message Emory might have relayed to Art regarding any sort of reprimand for her actions.

"And once I recovered my charge," Art continued, still he was not in a joking mode Cashmere could tell from him not seizing the opportunity to tease her further, "I could call 'Daddy'. Emory's words, not mine," Art added. It had grown weird between them, the forced explanations and words Art said hadn't felt wholly like his own. It wasn't like she was talking to Art at all, just a shell running on auto pilot while the real Art was somewhere deep- sulking, hiding, hurt, or fuming angry still, he could do nothing but be remote.

The guilt hit Cashmere all over again, "I'm sorry," she said and rushed forward, "Look if Emory isn't home, I'd rather just go home. I've probably ruined binge night."

"You're going to give me your address," Art asked with a slight perk to his voice, the remnants of the Art she knew somehow peaked through from just the idea of her address.

* * *

Cashmere saw an opportunity to make amends. No one knew where she lived outside of Emory and Dylan. She had her reason for that, reason's no one really questioned because it just became another of the other challenges, or mysteries if you asked Mike, about the band assistant. She reveled in her privacy which was why everyone was shocked when she opted to be on a reality tv show. What hadn't come to a shock to anyone was when she left it so quickly, because Cashmere wasn't the in your face type. She was a quiet type of flashy.

"No one else should know this," Cashmere smiled as she turned back to meet Art's gaze. "I mean it, I don't want any random band drop-ins once you know."

Art stared at Cashmere, "That won't be a problem."

Cashmere gave an awkward smile, Art's face seemed to be returning to some normalcy but the way he looked at her, his words, it still felt much too serious. She started to open her mouth to say something and lost her train of thought at the quick flicker of Art's eyes. She was sure she wasn't crazy. She was sure he'd flicked them to her lips and just as quickly went back to her eyes.

"I stay in Bella Norte," she started, "give me your phone and I'll enter my address."

Art hadn't questioned it, which was unusual but neither commented on that. Instead Art asked, "Didn't realize Stein paid you so well."

Cashmere knew, inevitably, a question of compensation would come up with where she lived and once she explained it wasn't based on her income she knew people would logically land on Emory. That was part of the problem.

Art, not one to be easily mislead, went straight in, "It's mostly Emory's isn't it?"

Cashmere shrugged, "Mostly," she confirmed. Art nodded and didn't press further. It was obvious of the roomies that Emory was the bread winner but even he had never really tried to understand the schematics of how the two came to live with each other and just how well they knew each other.

Cashmere wondered, in that moment, if she was still just the loner foster kid from the Midwest? Emory, despite all his posturing, never revealed this aspect about her to the show. It hadn't come up. They hadn't bothered. She was thankful.

As Art started the jeep there were questions that stirred and just as Siri started to recite the directions Cashmere said "Thank you." Art hadn't asked for what. And Cashmere never offered. The two fell back in silence as they pulled away from Art's place.

Everything had seemed to move so quickly. It was as though one moment they were at Art's, then in another flash they cruised down the Tré Jolla coast line, by the next instance they'd driven past the gates for the apartment Bel Nor complex, and now stared down the door to a cozy house.

Emory and Cashmere's home, to be exact it was Emory's place that Cashmere happened to stay at: This was how she preferred to frame it whenever her and Emory got in arguments over *their* place. As often as whenever the two were there at the same time for more than a few hours, which happened at the same frequency of finding a four-leaf clover, it had been part of the reason Emory tried convincing Cashmere to move in with him. He was barely home and the old girl, *their* home, could use the company. At least someone could take advantage of the lavish small digs.

Cashmere stuck her key into the hole just as Art joined her on the stoop, there wasn't a porch. At the start Cashmere couldn't find it in her to love a home without a porch but over time she began to enjoy the small garden that lined the walkway and the shrubs she'd planted beneath the windows. Cashmere caved pieces of her into the place, still, she wouldn't admit to it being 'their' place.

"Nice curb appeal," Art offered brushing against Cashmere, the contact causing a slight inhale before her breath leveled again. She was anxious to be in bed. It was definitely a lack of sleep that was making her mind spiral from one pointless guy to another but at least with Art she knew she had a kindred spirit when it came to trash television even if she might not be able to hang.

"Thanks," Cashmere mumbled as she pushed open the door and Art followed, "Home sweet home," she announced to the void, "excuse the mess." But there was no mess as they stepped into the living room where the only thing askew was a long red leather jacket draped across the cream loveseat, still in its clear dry-cleaning bag.

"This place is filthy," Art said coming behind Cashmere to lean into her ear and whisper, "You should be ashamed of yourself."

Cashmere hadn't dignified his sarcasm with a response instead she made a line toward the corridor and gave a tour in the process, "Kitchen" she said pointing to her right before she escaped down the hall, "Laundry, bathroom, Emory's room, my room, door to backyard and patio. You're welcome to use my bathroom if you want or Emory's, we pretty much stick to our own toilets but since we pretty much never have anyone over you can-"

"I claim the hall bathroom as mine!" Art exclaimed jumping into the frame of the open door and blocking it from entry. The light was still out. Cashmere half smiled, "Sure, just let me snag something from out of there."

"Snag or shag," Art wriggled his brow, the light returned to his features and it was as if the last several hours had not happened at all. They were able to just pick back up where they started, after the performance and have their night in with pizza. At the thought of food Cashmere's stomach made its own declaration.

"I don't have time for this," she said as she pushed past Art into the dark and stumbled over the shaggy rug, one of Emory's latest surprise additions, just as Art reached to grab hold of her. It happened quickly. The fall was cushioned by the rug and Art's disruption of gravity as he came down too.

"You're accident prone," Art huffed as he pressed his body upward. Cashmere unable to resist just how true his words were laughed uncontrollably; her hand came to rest on her forehead and a hiccup escaped. "Looks like someone's sleepiness has turned into deliria, I think I can get with that," Art joked as he dipped down to whisper something inappropriate in Cashmere's ear, just as she began to turn around and their lips touched. Except this time it hadn't been the same. They weren't at a gig, there was no male posturing, there was no one except the two and Cashmere immediately realized there was something more, with this kiss that she hadn't felt with Dallas. Something she couldn't put her finger on but that was real and tangible and at the moment she sighed her content at accepting it, her mouth opened and Art went in. He pressed into her inviting body.

Her hands gripped his hair, his back, and all the while she was aware of the dull ache emanating from between her thighs. One moment Art's body smothered Cashmere and by the next he was beneath her. Cashmere, for one brief second, was thankful for the large guest bathroom that made making out possible. She smiled into a kiss thinking how Emory might die a thousand deaths to know she made out on a bathroom floor, even if it was at his house, but she only gave the thought a moment. That was all her mind could do in between the heat rising and the sparing random thoughts that mostly centered around the impossibility of her and Art. Her and Art were never a thing. It's true they hung out often but this-

Cashmere pulled away. Gasping for a breath from a body that hadn't really wanted it to be caught, that hadn't desired to be stopped.

This isn't right.

We shouldn't do this.
What are we doing?
Okay, that was a good joke.

Cashmere thought words. Had words available but none of them made it past her filter.

But Art's had, and his was honest, she could tell, but it still hadn't felt right, even as he pressed breathlessly, "Why'd you stop?"

"I-"

And Art hadn't waited, he pushed off from the floor, Cashmere now straddled his lap and went straight for her lips. His hunger, his want hit her hard. There was something more, a desperation in the kiss that Cashmere was familiar with. There was more in the world than looking for the next lay. There were moments like these, moments that some had waited to happen.

Art's hand snaked around Cashmere's waist; he drew her closer to him. So close there was barely a wisp of air that escaped between their chests. His hands glided up her back and unclasped her bra without having to remove her top. The impressive move hadn't gone unnoticed. Cashmere had begun to smile when her mind, running wild as always, thought how he'd likely picked up the trick from the many women he'd been with. In fact, the there'd been the girl from earlier...

Cashmere pushed off and away. Her body collided with a wall in the dark as she scrambled up and flicked the bathroom light on. Art still on the floor, his hair more rumpled than usual, his lips delectable and his eyes- Cashmere turned away catching a glimpse of herself in the mirror. Her lips swollen, skin flushed, and already there was a hickey taking shape on her neck... *when did he?*

Art was up a moment later, his front to her back as she peered through the mirror. His eyes locked on hers. Already her body was deceiving her once more. She *felt* him as he pressed further. His lips dipped down to her neck, prepared to finish the mark he'd started, maybe give it a friend just as he took hold of her waist bringing her back against him, his lips descended, Cashmere's phone rang. She startled and backed away.

"I ca- We need to cool down," Cashmere announced. She sighed and knew she wouldn't be able to quickly shake off what had nearly happened. "I'm going to take that in my room," already she'd forgotten what she'd come to the bathroom to retrieve.

She knew she had to be away from Art though. "I'm also going to take a shower," *a very cold one*, "there's food in the fridge and some leftovers from dinner the other night or if you want to go grab something and I mean, if you can't or don't want to stay or I don't know. I mean it's okay. So, I'm fine and you should be fine. If you want to like leave or anything. For food I mean. Or if you want to, need to leave-leave. That's fine," Cashmere lost her train of thought the longer she stayed near Art. The longer she recognized nothing about his demeanor had changed. He still looked poised to pounce; his crotch still magnified by his still raging desire.

Art filled the door frame once more, both his arms pressed against the sides as he looked Cashmere in her eyes, "I'm claiming this."

Cashmere was sure he wasn't referring to the bathroom.

Chapter 12

Alexander

"Welcome esteemed chicks and sticks... Nope, again"

"Welcome ladies and bleh, start it over-"

"Welcome my fabulous pricks and dicks, for fucks sake shine that extra headlamp somewhere else. AGAIN!"

"Hello and good evening my lovelies- Yep that's it, that's the one. I'm not fit for too much color today," Rick said as he fanned himself, "I'm dying here, where are the fans or did we have to pawn those off too?"

Although he spoke in jest it was true the budget constraints were starting to make their presence known but with the spike in ratings and all the social media buzz it was going to aid some of the hurt. However, it would only be temporary if they couldn't figure out how to stop the bleeding. Who knew an online series could be so expensive Alexander sometimes wondered?

The next few episodes on the docket were okay at best. Qamar was cute but not memorable. Daisy had a knack for complaining and not in the way that steered the correct drama so she was out. Then there was Khloe who Rick had *tried* to help by offering her a pole class.

"What?! It's great exercise. Alexi would've loved it, isn't that right darling," Rick said as he batted his eyes that day at the reading. Khloe didn't go for it. *Alexi,* Alexander, wasn't interested in it either and now they were facing the day with a double elimination on the docket and a surprise that surfaced late last night/early morning while Alexander had been out. He was sure it came after his visit to Raquel who hadn't tried contacting him. It seemed better that way if he was being honest with himself.

And if he was being doubly honest with himself he was still worn out from a night of overthinking when it came to Cashmere. Then there was the charity event tonight...

He wanted this to be over, he was okay to lose the bet with himself, with Raquel by proving to her she'd been right all along. He wasn't sure what might come with Cashmere if anything at all but he wasn't anxious to sit around another week or two of daily eliminations and the whims of a crew that barely knew who was coming or going. Alexander was ready to get back to daily life, to a routine, a routine he hoped would include dates with Cashmere and getting to know her this time around. Unlike their first meeting which she'd never allowed him to live down.

"Alexi, honey, you awake over there? You look like death's rejected shadow. What gives? Are you struggling with the elimination tonight?" Rick asked and his brow perked. Alexander shook his head as he knew that Rick was probably hoping for a surprise. Every night Rick snuck a 'word to the wise' to Alexander and suggested he not follow along with project elimination. It was moment's like that which led Alexander to suspect that Rick might be the mole since some days it seemed he had the most at stake given the precariousness of his career and lack of gigs. He was an aging 'old Hollywood' host not ready to go out just yet.

Alexander yawned and shook off the sleep by sitting upright. He and Rick were in their usual overly large white wicker chairs for staging purposes. Rick claimed he needed Alexander's presence to help 'get him there' which always caused a snickered response from the cameramen but no one ever dared push Rick on his nonsense. So Alexander, well aware of how he appeared having stared down his brown-gray stubble ridden face and throwing on his glasses rather than contacts to hopefully distract everyone from the evident shadows, was doing his part despite slipping further and further away.

"The remaining ladies still vying passionately for her handsome bachelor and who wouldn't with his rugged 'I just rolled out of bed freshly fucked face courtesy of one Cashmere Watson. How was it finally?"

Alexander's eyes bulged as he turned, his mouth agape, and Rick's eyes twinkled with delight. "Am I dreaming right now or did I not hear you correctly?"

"Cash-mere Wat-son" Rick said slow, ensuring his lips enunciated each syllable, "Or that's the rumor and what Emory said."

"Emory wouldn't have said that."

"Well no, he said you were out looking for the curvy lady and your eyes suggest you found her. You found her allllll night long," and Rick's smile was devilish once again, "Think what the mention of her might bring. It's as though everyone WANTS to see you with her or Hannah. Personally, I think the idea of you and Porchia is a storyline that needs to be tapped into more."

"No," Alexander said abruptly, "Never again." He was still regretful of the night, their arrangement and now armed with the knowledge that Cashmere had been there, saw him, yet did nothing. Her silence spoke volumes. It was as though the two couldn't get right when it came to the other but each were perfectly content in their calculations in the show and in their escapes.

That was one of the things he missed most, going off to the place there were no cameras. The place that he and her were able to just let go and be without the need to play their roles. Him the stubborn asshole, her the feisty curvy vixen hell bent on disrupting any peace though part of Alexander still believed that maybe part of it hadn't been an act for her.

"No worries there. I believe you two are on the same page there unfortunately. Unless you have decided otherwise. So how is our misplaced vixen?" Rick asked just as he waved over a makeup artist. Katie and Ash both rushed over, both working on Rick as Alexander began to rise, reminded that he did want to find Emory.

"I don't know," Alexander answered honestly, "I'll let you know."

"No, no doll, where do you think you're going. We still need to talk about this afternoon?"

Alexander shrugged, "Do whatever works. You all hardly need my vote on the direction of this circus."

"Oh Alexi, you're so sexy when you're sleep deprived. Still itching for another fixing I take it? Must be good, you know, maybe we could work something out-"

"I'll be inside."

"But what about this afternoon? Are you okay with what they're planning to do?" Katie asked pausing from powdering Rick's face just as Ash came up as well to add, "Yeah, I would think you'd want to weigh in on the voting."

Alexander was already walking away having spotted Emory, he mumbled his apologies to Rick promising to catch up with whatever Jazmine had in mind later. Alexander knew he could inquire about all the pressing matters surrounding the afternoon with Emory if he wanted to but he was more interested in an update about Cashmere. He'd gone to Cashmere's and Emory's place late last night, no one answered. He'd tried Cashmere's phone again and still nothing.

"Emory," Alexander called out. He jogged leisurely across the lawn just as Emory stepped out and closed the sliding doors. Emory was on the phone and threw a finger up to Alexander then covered the mouthpiece, "trying to get the ducks in the row for tonight, what's wrong?"

"Cashmere." Just one word, the only one needed really and Emory rolled his eyes. Alexander wasn't sure if it was a result of the other person on the line or the fact, he should've known that'd be the thing that dragged him away from Rick, who could still be heard from across the lawn.

"Safe at home, sleeping it off," Emory smiled then proceeded to walk away. It hadn't escaped Alexander's eyes that there'd been a hesitation, a look that passed across Emory's face.

Alexander caught Emory by the shoulder, "Do you need me?"

"I don't need you," Emory said as he made a quick exit down the steps and walked across the lawn toward Rick who jumped at the sight of Emory.

Alexander observed the exchange and it was at odds with how the two normally were with each other but he hadn't cared. Nothing really mattered anymore if he could have a chance to talk his idea with Cashmere. He was ready to give it up, break the contract if there was even a slight part of her that might be willing to see. That was all Alexander needed. He had the hope; he just required the spark to set the place ablaze.

Alexander had always believed it hadn't mattered what time of the day you traveled; some highways were always jam packed, but he knew better. In traveling the half hour trip to Emory and Cashmere's place, turned hour due to an accident, the thought to turn back around had never crossed Alexander's mind even as he pulled into the driveway and saw another vehicle there.

He knew it wasn't Emory's as he'd just left him sidelined with an arm's flailing Rick. It wasn't possible for Emory to have beaten Alexander here unless the rumors were true. And the rumors were Emory didn't need sleep because he was a vampire which was sound in comparison to the rumor that Emory was the black Batman.

Walking up the short-decorated path from the sidewalk to the door it hadn't crossed Alexander's mind to give pause. That maybe, just maybe the woman he'd spent the night worrying about might not be alone. He rang the doorbell, his fist pounded on the door for only a moment before the door swung open with a man with ruffled hair and in nothing but boxers as he opened the door on a yawn. He hadn't recognized him instantly but he knew the guy seemed familiar. He was just hoping he didn't seem familiar for reasons that involved Cashmere in deeply intimate ways. He ran back there many conversations in the storage closet adjacent back room but nothing came to mind. This guy definitely wasn't Dallas. And it was the name that triggered the placement.

"Art?" Alexander asked surprised to see the lead guitarist for MAADD Maxi here but now that he thought it about. He was sure he remembered Cashmere mentioning that her and Art were the television binge watchers of the group. And maybe technically she was working, band assistant, but it seemed too early for her to already be working. And why was he in only his boxers looking as though... Looking the way he had. Alexander was poised to answer the question when Art's face seemed to have it's own moment of recognition.

At first Art's eyes had narrowed shortly before lifting again which was strange because Alexander was sure he knew who he was. Deciding to not linger on the odd reaction Alexander smiled, "Art," he repeated, this time with less emphasis of questioning or wander in his voice, "how have you been? You guys' website still holding up well?"

Art, true to his nature smiled a goofy smile and ruffled his hair some more, "Alexander, my man, morning and good day to you sir. The website is handling most awesomely. You're the best."

Alexander smiled. "Very good to know."

"Anytime," Art said, not offering anything more. The two stood before with nervous smiles on their face. Art not moving any further and Alexander not sure where to go.

"I'm looking for Cashmere," Alexander said as he remembered he was the one outside his terrain having come to pay her a visit. It would be a bit more awkward with Art here but Alexander was past being concerned with everyone else.

Art's eyes narrowed again and this time there was no mistaking that there was something behind the look. "Hey, so if Emory sent you here to try to convince Cashmere she's not doing it. Not cool man, I didn't think you'd be like that after all that."

Art hadn't waited for an answer as he began to close the door when Alexander's hand reached out, "hold it Art, what are you talking about? Emory didn't send me here on some secret mission. I'm here to see Cashmere of my own accord. I need to talk to her about something important."

Art raised a brow, not believing Alexander, it seemed to him at least so he held a hand up, "Honestly Art I come in peace. I really just want to talk to Cassi- Cashmere. I tried getting hold of her last night and even came by but she wasn't here. And technically I am here because of Emory, but that's only because he knew I spent half the night awake waiting to hear from her. She still hasn't returned any of my messages."

"Technical difficulties," Art said nodding, "she sort of had an accident since being home that involved her phone and the shower. I think B.O.B. wasn't working out and the alcohol was still in her system," Art joked but Alexander hadn't laughed.

"Is it possible for you to go get her or let me in if she's indisposed at the moment? I can wait," Alexander asked taking a step forward.

Art moved toward the outside, blocking Alexander. They stood eye to eye. It was then Alexander noticed that the two were the same height but mannerisms were completely opposite. Alexander was older, in his earlier thirties compared to Art who was more suited for Cashmere's age range. Not intending to Alexander found himself comparing the fine, zero gray mane of Art's to the image of his own from the morning.

"No can-do chief. Cashmere's done with that world and while I don't think you're here for any sneak attacks to get her to come back on the show my girl needs her rest. She had a bit of a wild night," Art's eye sparkle and if it weren't for the fact Alexander had a conversation with Emory regarding said 'wild night' he might suspect the sexual undertones. But seeing as Art likely doesn't know that Alexander had a conversation with Emory it's become clear to Alexander that Art meant to lead him on. The 'my girl' sentiment was not lost to Alexander either.

There were multiple routes, answers that Alexander could pursue. He could let Art in on the fact that he was well aware of Cashmere's temporary disappearance but to do so could result in a pissing match. It was clear that Art was standing as guard dog for more than just Cashmere's interest. Alexander's held back his own desire to take on a defensive stance. Best to play Art's game a little while longer and hope Cashmere emerged.

"Sounds like she survived it though."

"She did and now her body is all banged out you know. I could leave a message for when she gets up. You probably need to hurry back to the show, right?"

Alexander's phone decided to sound at that precise moment, just as he accepted the call, he saw Art's body backing away from the frame. "Good luck," Art yelled before slamming the door shut.

"That was loud," Raquel said, "And hello! What do you need good luck for? End of days in bizzaro world?"

Alexander eyes were still firmly fixed on the door, not sure what kept him mounted in place aside from the answer that threatened to spill out if he dare knock on the door again and it be answered by Art.

"Hello, you over there *Alexi*?" Raquel said with a laugh. "I hear breathing, heavy breathing? Tired from lifting your finger and pointing? Life's hard right."

"Not now Raquel."

"It not now, then when dear, we only have this moment, the next isn't guaranteed and blah blah blah some mumbo jumbo, CRAP!" Raquel screamed as the sounds of pots clattering erupted across the line.

"Maybe you should call me back."

"Or maybe you should join me for some lemonade and a beach-scape as the day is too beautiful to not be soaking up."

"Can't do, busy."

"But Alexi- I'm bored. It's beautiful. You're beautiful. I'm beautiful. Why can't me you and our beautiful sky weather kid make more beauty together. Why not make the world sick with our beauty? Why not make them watch from afar and say things like 'That's gross, that's just too much beautiful in one place, they should be ashamed of themselves, where's the damn police. I can't stand it this beaut-"

"Raquel. You're stalling," Alexander said taking a tentative step backward away from Cashmere's door. There was still a force holding him. It was true he was probably due back on set with this uproar over the afternoon and evening eliminations. While he hadn't prepared to spend a lot of time with Cashmere he definitely hadn't expected to walk away without any answer. Even still there was some force, some draw that whispered to him *not yet* and so he took slow steps backward but he hadn't given up his view of her door.

"You're right I am. I got a call from your crazy show with a proposal. A desperate one at that and I was thinking about what you said. I've been thinking about it a lot actually," Raquel admitted and Alexander detected something in her voice he wasn't used to hearing, it almost seemed sad but it wasn't possible. Raquel prided herself on being Ms. Realistic after all.

Alexander stopped and breathed in the Cali air. He closed his eyes just as two things happened.

"I think I might take them up on the offer to compete. Throw a wrench in the competition but also maybe I've been wrong about you, about us. I think my reaction last night and today, maybe I'm not ready for this to be over," she said the last part in a whisper just as Cashmere opened her door.

Alexander noted Art was standing behind, none too thrilled to see him still there. He smiled. Not for Art, but he hoped Art got the wrong impression and took it as smugness on his part even though it hadn't been.

No, there was something quiet taking place amongst Alexander's heart and mind at the appearance of the sensuous curves of Cashmere as she stood in only pink short shorts and a red camisole, her hair haphazardly bundled on top of her head. Her beautifully wavy brown hair with hints of blonde, it hadn't seemed wet from a shower but she looked dressed for bed no doubt. Their eyes met and Cashmere smiled. Alexander returned. It appeared to him that she'd been taking him in as well, as if she could hardly believe it. Alexander, if he could be sure of her thoughts might have even confirmed not believing it either.

"Hey Ernie," she mouthed to him.

"Hey Cass," he returned to her and he stepped forward hanging up his phone, he'd stopped hearing Raquel.

"Hey Stranger," Cashmere said audibly.

"Me? Stranger? Okay, Ms. I Like To Party All the Time"

"Not all the time, just in the early morning hours when I should be sleep and dreaming about pink and purple unicorns."

Alexander laughed, "Still chasing after them huh?"

"They're just too fast and the rainbow and butterfly fart are pretty damn distracting."

"Still a devil horned frog playing the loveliest sound known to the human ear."

"Indeed," Cashmere said just as Alexander made it to standing within five feet of her, "You were worried."

"I was. I am." Alexander's phone rang again. He took a quick glance and noticed it wasn't Raquel calling back but Jazmine instead.

Cashmere took notice of the name, "Answer it," she said, "But don't tell her you're with me."

Alexander laughed and nodded. "Hey Jazz."

"Are you with Cashmere?"

Alexander turned an eye back to Cashmere but she only winked and turned around to talk to Art. Art was stiff and it was obvious to Alexander he wasn't happy to have him still around as the seconds ticked by.

"What's up," Alexander asked, pretending to not hear her question. Lucky for him Jazmine wasn't interested in pursuing it.

"Whatever, Emory will have to cross that bridge. We needed you hear twenty minutes ago. Tell me that wherever you are that you can be back in the next ten minutes. Please tell me you're not far. PLEASE tell me you're on your way back."

"Okay, I'm on my way back," he agreed, "But I'm not going to be there in ten minutes."

"Fine, just get here now or risk this blowing up more than you or I care to deal with."

Alexander didn't have a chance to answer back. Jazmine was gone and he sighed. The conversation with Cashmere would have to wait. Maybe it was for the best with Art being around.

Cashmere was just walking back toward Alexander. She was a sight for sore eyes. He wanted to imprint that casual sway she had and come back to it every time the day tried to bring him down.

"I have to go."

She smiled, "I figured as much. Jazz doesn't just call unless it's serious."

"Can we talk later? Make time for me please? Just us," Alexander tacked on flicking his eyes in the general direction of Art before having them land back on Cashmere's.

"Later," Cashmere confirmed and closed the distance reached up to give Alexander a hug, "Good luck with tonight. I hear it's a double. Still sticking to the plan?"

Alexander nodded from within her embrace. Taking in her scent like it was the last time. For all he knew it very well could be as he remembered Raquel's words. "We are, but everyone is talking about some afternoon plan. Trying to save the ratings that are doing well but could be *'better'*," Alexander said as he thought to keep his mouth in check. The part that said he wasn't afraid of starting something he'd gladly finish.

She kissed his cheek. "Good luck Ernie," she whispered in his ear.

"I'll do my best. See you at the charity event tonight," he said confirming their agreement to talk.

Cashmere shook her head, "We'll see."

"Later." Alexander wanted to linger further but jogged to his car instead, started it up, beeped a couple times as he pulled away and watched as Cashmere shrank in his rearview. He also watched as Art moved in, in his absence. The sight bothered him more than it should but the quickest way to solve for that would be having a talk with Art once Alexander had the chance to talk to Cashmere. To lay it all out.

"I'm ready," he smiled all the way back to the set, even when stuck in traffic. There was nothing that could bring him down. At least he thought there wasn't until he arrived over an hour later and found a despondent Jazmine sitting in a hall going over the camera angle with a Set Runner.

"Too late," Jazmine said eyeing Alexander as he walked up.

Alexander began to open his mouth when he watched Xandra emerge from a bathroom, "Alexander," the beautiful blonde said excitedly. She placed a deft peck on both his cheeks before moving onward, "Wonderful idea," she called back just as a makeup artist sprinted by to catch up with her.

Alexander mind fumbled for a response. Jazmine put it out of its misery, "They're all back except-"

"Cashmere" they said in unison. Jazmine continued "But Emory just left, he's working on that. Go to room 5, Ash is waiting for you there and don't say I didn't warn you. I tried but I'm just one person."

Jazmine walked away. Another stagehand grabbed her before she could make it a few feet down the hall.

Alexander slumped against the wall. All signs indicated this day wasn't going to end well. He shot a quick text to Cashmere hoping she'd get it before Emory arrived.

Chapter 13

Cashmere

"Hey are you still going to take this shower or not?" Cashmere asked emerging from her bedroom as she yelled down the hall. She'd just had the fifth conversation with Emory. Already the house line was ringing and she sighed. "By the way who was at the door?"

Art was slow to turn around but when he did his face was all smiles, "Didn't know you guys got Jehovah Witnesses out this way."

Cashmere wrinkled her nose, "Me neither, then again I'm usually tied up with you guys during the day so maybe they finally saw movement and took a chance. Plus that big hunk of a red machine just exudes 'people home.'"

Art laughed shaking his head. "I'll take that."

"You should, now go shower because you're wasting my hot water and if I knew you were going to delay like that, I wouldn't have bothered running it for you. Hey by the way, were you able to fix my phone?"

"Oh yeah," Art said handing Cashmere back her cellphone, "I factory reset it and wiped everything out."

"Why? There was a message from Alexander on here. I wanted to listen to it."

"You could have but it's pretty clear he and Emory have tagged up to try to get you back on the show. And after that long ass bitch fest not too long ago I got the impression you were over it."

"There was no bitch fest," Cashmere uttered as she rolled her eyes and walked over to the window to retrieve a blanket. "Remind me to never give you actor commentary again when we're watching anything with me involved in it."

Art winked, "Oh but I love your commentary. Don't punish me for my honesty."

"Consider yourself punished," she said as she snuck a peek outside and movement from the white transparent drape caught her attention. She sucked in a breath.

"You want to make that shower even hotter by joining me," Art said, closer to Cashmere than she realized. She backed into him as she rushed to rise, mumbling an apology as she ditched the blanket and rushed over to the door. "Where's the fire?" Art asked as he readjusted himself. Cashmere tried to pay no mind to him as she swung the door open. There was a little part of her surprised that Emory dared give him the address but there he was standing facing her with a grin on his unshaven face.

His thick black rimmed frames did little to conceal the dark circles that haunted his eyes. She knew he'd been awake for hours; he was making another call, probably one of many he'd made throughout the night, because one moment the phone was at his ear and by the next he was off it.

For one solid moment it was simply Cass and Ernie. That moment was theirs alone.

Twenty minutes had passed since Alexander had left. Art eventually made his way to the shower, the water cold by then but he still stuck it out far longer than Cashmere would have imagined. He hadn't joked about her joining him. His eyes betrayed him but the return on his somber mood was one that Cashmere hadn't wished to explore. She had her suspicions but she was sure it was probably best to not pursue any ventures that might disrupt the harmony of the band. Cashmere was settling on the couch with a large bowl of popcorn when her phone went off signaling a text. Then another directly after it.

One was from Emory –

> OMW. Forgot keys. We need to
> talk.... Betta let me in :P

The other from Alexander. Cashmere's stomach fluttered. At the sight of his name a small smile tickled the corner of her lips as she opened it-

> Emory's headed there. Need to
> talk son.

She smiled, positive he meant 'soon'. But the idea of Alexander channeling some 90's slang had tickled her.

It seemed the last 24 hours had been plagued by boys of both past, present, and future. Her crush on Dallas, part of the past that she'd exorcised from her body through one kiss, and a confirmed slut move on his part. He wasn't the one. She'd always known it but it felt good to be at a place to be at one with that idea.

Then there was Art. Art had come from out of nowhere and yet he hadn't. It seemed had she opened her eyes sooner regarding Dallas she might've been able to take notice at what was already standing in front of her and recognized the potential of it.

And finally there was Alexander. Their first meeting years ago when he came to work on a project for the band hadn't gone over smoothly but in the short span she'd been on the show it appeared that the two were wrong about the other. Both vowed that once the show was over, no matter how it eventually played out, they'd make it being friends and catch a Padres game together. Cashmere was lazily dreaming away the game and the shared supreme nachos when Art came out with nothing but his hand cupping his member.

"Did you take my boxers?" He accused. There was a hint of annoyance in his tone but it hadn't lasted long as his eyes narrowed, "What's your game Watson?"

"OMG! For fuck's sake you could've just used the towel."

"What towel?!"

"I put a, I mean there should've been a towel on the rack," Cashmere said as she bolted up from the couch nearly sending the large bowl of popcorn flying. "I figured you wanted me to wash them. I laid out an extra pair of Emory's jersey shorts for you with a towel, I mean they were," Cashmere started as she reached the quickly vanishing steamy confines of the cooled bathroom, "I sat them on the toilet." Not waiting around for Art's quip she walked the few steps to Emory's room, flicked the light on and there on his dresser were the items she'd pulled out for Art to use temporarily.

"That was a convenient spot," Art said from the door where he was poised against it and his arms crossed. Momentarily forgetting his nakedness for the sake of taking on an 'I told you so' pose to Cashmere. It wasn't until her eyes bulged that he realized his form. "Sorry," he said with the grace to blush. "So used to being on the right side of things."

Cashmere nodded and left him to the light blue tropical themed bedroom. Cashmere had decorated it as such on a bet she'd won between her and Emory. It wasn't often she won but she relished the times she had. *'You're so distracting yourself right now...'* Cashmere thought.

"It's too big," Art called out.

"That's what Bey said," Cashmere returned.

"It's too big, it's too strong, it won't fit- talk like this cuz I can back it up," Art said tossing himself on the couch and flipping over the bucket of popcorn. Cashmere sighed.

"I'm not making anymore." She wrapped the blanket around her more and flicked on the television, but she wasn't able to lose herself and find something to binge. There were a set of eyes that bore into her making it impossible to do much else. "Why are you staring?"

"Was just thinking how fate works sometimes. Spend so much of your time trying to deny yourself something and sit back watching that something desire another, another much less knowing she's so valuable."

"You're not beating around the bush much," Cashmere joked turning to Art but his eyes were solemn and round. There was no light dancing about.

"I think I've done that enough. You're finally seeing past chasing Dallas for what it is, you get off that show, and the illusion of an opening is there but it's just that an illusion because something, without a doubt always-"

BOOM BOOM BOOM

"OPEN UP CASHMERE! I KNOW YOU'RE IN THERE!"
Emory walked over to the window and tapped his car key against it. It was then Cashmere noticed she'd misplaced her phone but it had only sunk into a cushion. On it were a few texts from Emory.

> Almost there

> Unlock the door, should be there in five.

> Let me in.

Cashmere got up to open the door when Art mumbled, "Always something interrupting."

She pretended not to hear as she began to open the door but suddenly realized she might be setting herself up for a sinking ship. Emory always got his way and if there was some green lit project of his in jeopardy without her presentation, well, she knew he'd do anything to make it happen. Even at the expense of their friendship which was most often the case.

The two were more borderline frenemies some days than actual friends. Emory often willed his ideas onto Cashmere until she eventually caved and did his bidding. It was one of the reasons she was anxious to get out and find a place of her own before there was no friendship to return to.

Not opening the door Cashmere yelled to Emory, "Is it about the show?"

"Of course! Now open the damn door before I call the police and have to get all Bruce Lee on you."

There was another reason Cashmere stalled with letting Emory in, more than anything his OCD might kick in and the room was slightly askew, plus peppered with popcorn, since his last visit. She needed to do some quick remediation. To Art she pointed and made a sweeping motion with her hand to indicate the popcorn that needed to be swept up.

"Now really isn't a good time. Can we talk about the show some other time?"

"Yeah some of us were trying to enjoy a little bit of afternoon delight before our *dessert dinner*. Cashmere does wonders with her lips," Art said.

"You and all your dirty jokes," she started, beginning the mental ticker, a count of Art's direct and indirect sexual innuendos. It was a thing she did when around the band.

"Look I'm not game for whatever shenanigans or conquest you two think you'll achieve by screwing about but I need to get in and we HAVE to talk Cashmere. Now either we can do this the hard way or I'll have Art physically remove you from blocking the door," Emory said.

"And how exactly will you do that? I hold the power," Cashmere said without an ounce of belief in her own bravado. Before Cashmere had a chance to gage Art's own reaction to Emory's threat she was already being removed from the door. Art appeared dejected as he gently moved Cashmere away from the door, undid the chain lock and allowed Emory to step in. The warm weather breached the cool of the house's central air. At least the air wasn't humid but the fact she was even getting hit with the air was bothersome. Something had instantly shifted and she hadn't been sure why but she sensed a shared emotion when Art did lift his eyes to Cashmere. She instantly recognized the slight fear there.

Was it possible, like her, that Emory too had something on Art? Something worth Art letting him in and not playing along, allowing her to stall. At least Art had gotten the popcorn up but it probably wouldn't have mattered as Emory's mouth hit the floor, "what'd you do! I never signed on to rearranging. We agreed we'd always talk about any major moves."

"Well I tried," Cashmere whined crossing her arms and flopping over to the loveseat instead of returning to the couch where Art now sat, with his feet on the coffee table until Emory used a magazine to swipe them away. "I'm barely out the door and already you've staked claim on this place like you're the damned Queen of Sheeba. What the hell Cashmere? We agonized over this and you turn it inside out within a mere day."

"Emory," Cashmere started her voice low. She wasn't anxious to get her mind there but if Emory was insistent on focusing on the arrangement of the furniture, she was prepared to go into her own overdrive crazy mode even if it meant doing so in front of company. "You've barely lived here in the last year. I was tired of looking at the place a certain way and decided on a change after I got the boot from the show. So it's not been like this very long at all. And I planned on talking to you about it once you got past the latest crux. It's a fucking room. It didn't seem worth troubling you over, geesh."

Emory's eyes narrowed as he chewed on his bottom lip, "So you were pissed from getting the boot, took it out on me and my place? Real nice Cashmere."

This was the point of the conversation where things could either escalate or go down but it was always contingent on how

Cashmere proceeded because she couldn't expect Emory to immediately see the error of his ways. No, she had always been the one to cave first and this time would be no different. She was ready for change. She was ready to move on from the oppressive ties of Emory and his house and his rules. The more Cashmere thought about it, the more she was sure her next move didn't mean choosing a guy in her love life. It meant getting away from the toxicity that Emory sometimes invoked. They could be fine together but the truth was friends didn't blackmail friends and Cashmere suspected Emory might be up to just that if he didn't get his way.

Rather than answer Emory. Cashmere stalked off to her room and packed her overnight duffle bag. She'd come for the rest later. She no longer wanted to be here despite many of the touches to the place was her own and while she enjoyed having a roommate, it wasn't meant to be for her and Emory. Returning from her room with the duffle bag she announced, "Look I'm going to watch a bit of tv, wait for Art's clothes to finish, then we're leaving. I'll get you back your keys Em, but after that I'm gone. I'll work with you for the rest of the week to get the rest of my clothes and free up your space. This is it."

Emory eyed her warily. "You're not serious and frankly I'm not even sure why you're entertaining it. You have nowhere to go unless you're heading back to KC. Stop acting like an indignant child, hear me out."

"I'd rather not. You've made it clear that this friendship is based on 'what shit I can blackmail Cashmere with today' and I'm sick of it Emory. It was fun to begin with but the constant manipulation is bull. And frankly I'm too damn tired to even have this argument so screw leaving, I'm paid through to the end of the month I'm going to bed. Art," Cashmere said turning her attention to the guitarist in Emory's clothing, which Emory had yet to notice, "I'm not sure what kind of crap Emory has on you and it's obvious he does I understand if you can't suddenly help me.In fact if you need to leave now just take your clothes and run. I'm tired of the world right now." Without any formal warning Cashmere sauntered off to her room forgetting the shows she'd had in queue.

Cashmere flicked on the lights to her bedroom, slammed the door and locked it shut. With her phone in hand she jumped onto the bed and fired a text to Alexander.

> I'm ready too.

Chapter 14

Two Years Earlier

In his dream Alexander was in the room with the woman dressed as a bumble bee except she no longer wore the dress. She was dressed in a simple pink camisole and silk polka dot pajama bottoms. She whispered into his ear, "Trying to make a girl feel special are we?" Alexander's face heated but he didn't reply because for now it's just nice to not have to put on a show. She tells him her real name, the birth name because this is what they decide will be their thing. It'll later be the thing that they have to prove to each other.

"Ernest," he told her. "My real name is Ernest Alexander. They added the Roth."

"Mmm… Alexander E. Roth does sound cooler. Makes you seem more important than you actually are."

"That's because I am," and they both share a laugh. In the dream her laughter was what he sought. "I don't want to wake up."

"You're still lying about your name. Who you are… what you want…"

Her eyes were on him, her thoughts her own, he can't hear them in the dream but he's read her face and can tell she'll say the words that'll unravel them both.

"Let's hide here forever."

His smile was there before her she'd finished, "…If only."

He's said this before and she nodded. "Have to face the music at some point."

Alexander moved in closer, not sure why he did but knew it felt appropriate. Warmth flooded his body as she mirrored his movement until there was barely a space between them.

"You have to say yes first," she said, "If you don't-"

beep beep beep

beep beep beep

"How long has he been sleep now?" A familiar voice asked.

beep beep beep

"Don't forget to say yes," she reminded him, the woman from his dreams, the bumblebee lady.

"Bumblebee Lady," he muttered from his semi-conscious state.

"How long has he been out," the familiar voice asked. Having heard the voice there was an ease that settled over his body but it was a different, there were other feelings attached to the voice, none of them malice but there was an edge of insecurity. A fear that reflected a potential need, a need afraid to be met because there was hurt that surrounded it.

"He took a pretty nasty hit to the head," said another voice, "Do you want to come back in the morning? Are you aware of any immediate family that you might want to contact or inform his job so no missing person's report get entered."

"No, it's only me" the familiar voice said. The words took Alexander back, back to the dream where the bumblebee was. And she was still there when he returned except, she was dressed differently.

"What's your deal, dude?" She said her eyes narrowed as she hunched over a computer monitor. It was then Alexander noticed the person sitting at the desk, the back of the head he was looking at was his own.

"What's your name," Alexander asked as he stepped closer.

He watched as 'dream Alexander' swiveled in the desk chair, a scowl on his stubble face, "Not your concern. Just remember to say yes."

"Yes to what?"

"Just say yes," they answered in unison. Alexander jumped at the impact of their words. Her eyes softened.

"We'll get it right Ernie. Ernie. Ernie. *Ernie…. Ernie…*"

Alexander felt his mind slipping again. The foggy feeling of being beckoned to one place, while perfectly content elsewhere. An overwhelming lethargic weight- that came with the task of returning where he was being called to versus staying there with the Bumblebee.

"Ernie, can you hear me," his hand was grasped firm, his own figures felt loose and nimble. He wasn't sure he knew what he wanted to do with them other than grip back but it seemed to require effort that his mind could not put forth toward.

"Ernie," the voice said, caught on a hitch. It was the pain laced in it that made him look one final time at the Bumblebee. She smiled a sad smile. She knew his decision even before he had, as if she had known all along that it would never be her. It was a smile of acceptance. It was sadness. It was her saying it was okay. But really, for Ernie, it hadn't felt okay. It hadn't felt okay at all.

"I still love you," the pained voice whispered. A vision was appearing before and as it tried to come into focus another faded. Bumblebee was going. The version of him at the desk already lost to his weakened state of mind. It hadn't occurred to Alexander to question what might be happening, why this strange feeling of being two places at once, in two different realities at separate times. He hadn't known as he came more and more aware. The dream was already leaving him. The things he experienced quickly sunset to the recesses of his fuzzy mind. He was forgetting. But also remembering the girl dressed as a Bumblebee, the blind date, the cyclist, and then the nothing.

The dream was gone. Bumblebee remained but he hadn't known what to do with her. Already he'd forgotten her face. How was it possible for something to be so sharp in a dream, only moments ago, to already be gone when waking? He knew if he ever came across her again he'd known her. Somehow, he too, suspected she would be able to do the same thing. They had crossed paths before. Alexander was a believer in fate, that everything happened for a reason. There was a reason the Bumblebee girl found him in his drug induced sleep. *Was he drugged?* He wasn't quite sure

Just like there had been a reason for the incident today he was sure there was a reason he found his ex-fiancé in a hospital chair beside his bed holding his hand, mumbling his name. It couldn't be some random reason for her to be here.

He thought about waking Raquel but she seemed at peace. Her dark hair draped across his bed. He hadn't seen her sleeping this quietly in some time. He resisted the urge to caress her face or move her hair away. He loved her still. He imagined there would always be some part that loved her but the break had taught him something, something she might not had intended but something he'd learned nonetheless.

When you say you're ready, oftentimes, you are ready but if the other person isn't then maybe there's a reason for that. Raquel had tried to point this out to him. And maybe she had been right all along.

There was only one way to know for sure. He couldn't recall why, or where it'd come from, maybe it was a result of the bump to the head but Raquel had once proposed he throw his name in as a contender for one of the many pilots that were greenlit. Raquel was working in the legal department for a major television network and questions came up often. What started off as a joke at the time didn't seem to have much bearing but then Raquel called off their engagement. He'd always accused her of being the unsure one, too nervous, too stubborn to admit she was her own problem.

Raquel was smart and now Ernie could recognize what she wanted him to realize with the promise of forever. Maybe the bump on the head had driven him into madness but her idea no longer seemed crazy. All he could think of was saying 'yes' when she woke.

Yes, she was right.

Yes, forever is a huge commitment.

Yes, he could prove his love to her or-

Yes, prove she was right on this front as well.

Yes, he thought, *yes*, I'll try .

Alexander's hand tightened around Raquel as he drifted back to sleep with dreams of sugar plum fairies and dancing bumblebees.

Two hours later Cashmere had finally worked out an excuse. She was still going to be running on time for the gig but she was worn out from the happy hour gathering. This was going to be the last time she double booked her social/work calendar. She still needed to run back home and do a wardrobe change out as she wasn't too excited to be near a mosh pit in a skirt. There was also the matter of talking logistics with Emory. She'd been with him for a few months already, and already she was seeing that there would be problems.

She longed to be home again but there was not much of a home to return to now that she was the only one. Not having known her biological parents all she had were adoptive ones and they were long gone. Her grandparents who'd practically raised her too had transitioned. In some ways Emory was her only relative seeing as they were both from the same small town. He'd made it work and had become successful but Emory had family there. This was his home first before his Dad decided to move somewhere quiet to allow Emory's mom time to recover from Treatment. Emory came from money whereas Cashmere hadn't.

Per the usual Emory wasn't home when Cashmere arrived and she did her usual note of 'we need to talk' and left it at that. It did no good to elaborate, it actually made it worse.

A sure way to get Emory's attention was mess. Stepping into their home Cashmere began kicking off her heels, grabbing hold the hem of her black and white skirt to tug it down, it landed with a whoosh onto the cream couch, then came her yellow top that she disposed down the hall in route to her bedroom. She'd just started to unhook her bra when a very loud bang against the wall caused her to jump. It'd come from Emory's room. Cashmere grabbed the bat from the hall closet, rushed down the hall in only her underwear and swung the door open to Emory's room which was pitch black. She distinctly saw two shadows moved and upon flicking on the light it was Emory.

"Oh!" Cashmere quickly shut the door. Emory was in there with his latest conquest which appeared to be an older white man: his latest male preference as he'd just gotten over his Bear phase. The man, probably in his late thirties or early forties appeared familiar to Cashmere but she hadn't been sure why.

"You two have fun, stay out of trouble," Cashmere yelled outside the door, still slightly and walked back toward her room to hopefully find something that was classy enough for a late gig but still appropriate concert attire. She wanted fun. She wanted comfortable. She wanted professional. She wanted that all wrapped up in something simple that wouldn't require much effort or at least would give the look that it'd been thrown together.

She wanted to pass out just from the thought alone. It was tiring to think of her wardrobe having just one outfit that encompassed and embodied the look she was going for. Cashmere knew she'd have to let go of something, if not for the mosh pit she would have been fine sporting a skirt but the idea of being around a drunk crowd in a skirt wasn't appealing. Cashmere wasn't looking for any 'accidental' molestations, people tended to feel at liberty with the body that either surfed or got flung around within the mosh pit. She was okay with not being included in the violated tally.

After about half an hour of putting around in her closet. Cashmere finally landed on shiny leather capris, a thin light blue blouse, and thin jacket since she tended to be sensitive about the flab from her arms. She knew it was mostly in her head but that didn't stop her from throwing on a jacket every once in a while even if the weather would be intent on making her regret her self consciousness flaw.

Cashmere strolled out of her room and found Emory on the couch with a blanket. "Where's your friend?"

"Ran to the store for some supplies," Emory answered, his attention firmly fixed on the television. Cashmere hadn't recognized what he was watching but was wary in asking. If it was something Emory was sucked into it'd likely turn into an hour discussion that involved the details of the show, plot, his theories, and any other relevant information regarding the world of the show. Normally Cashmere indulged him in his rambles but to do so would jeopardize her ability to be on time for once. She desperately wanted to be on time for this. She intended to prove to the band, specifically the manager, her talents were needed and could be of value overall. That and she wanted to quit her day job. Being full time in her band assistant role had its benefits since she got paid a set amount even if it didn't amount to the number of hours in the contract. That way, the manager figured, when things were heavy it'd balance out but so far it was in Cashmere's favor.

"Supplies," Cashmere noted. She had no interest in what sort of supplies because again, knowing Emory, it would go into territory she had no time for. Instead she felt stalled. Now was her chance. She wondered if Emory had observed the note she'd left earlier, if he had, he wasn't saying anything but that didn't mean he hadn't. It also meant, or could mean, that Emory was stalled much like Cashmere. She sighed and her phone began to ring. She hit ignore by accident missing the number. A text followed by, "WHERE ARE YOU?

"Rick thinks you have a face for television. Looks like you're in a hurry but he wanted me to tell you that," Emory said as he looked at Cashmere. There was something behind those eyes she noticed but nothing she could address because apparently something had changed.

"Is that your friend's name? Rick?" She asked as she stepped toward the door, stopping to grab a handful of kettle popcorn from Emory's bowl, that was his favorite snack as he watched shows.

"Yeah, you've seen him before," Emory shrugged. "At any rate he has an idea for a show and is trying to get it greenlit now. He's over to talk through the details of it."

"Right, talk through it. Looks like there's plenty of talking going on," Cashmere said as she opened the door.

"Har har," Emory said, "By the way, clean up your damn mess when you get back. I don't know what you think this is but we ain't gotz no maid," Emory said with a roll of his head and air snapping his fingers. Cashmere laughed. He smiled. This was definitely her favorite version of Emory.

Chapter 15

Alexander

Sometimes I wish we could just be strangers again...

It wasn't the first time Alexander had read the words and he was sure it wouldn't be his last. As he closed the journal containing the letter he heard the rustle that signaled he was no longer alone. Today was his last day.

He couldn't say he'd missed the place considering how much more was missing from him...

"You ever wake up and feel like there's a chunk of you missing?"

"Can't say that I have," the nurse responded.

"Yeah, me neither," Alexander said as he adjusted himself to a sitting position and drank more of the juice with a straw that was too big.

He was on the brink of drifting once more when a knock came at the door. Of course it was her. She smiled as she nodded to the nurse. No sooner had she taken a seat had the nurse left.

"He's cute," Raquel said as she sat a duffle bag down, "He's a keeper."

Alexander's brow furrowed. It'd been two days and he still hadn't remembered much. There was a lot of worry over his memory loss but none quite like his own. On the contrary it was an odd feeling that he hadn't felt panicked. Instead there was a peace that washed over him.

Sure he'd spent the first twenty four hours having a mental freak out of sorts – he and Raquel still not together? No surprise. No longer at the firm? Surprising a bit but he'd wanted to quit and apparently he finally had. Participation in a reality show for the sake of love? Well, he could understand that a bit... if he had that missing time returned.

"So how'd you think you did?" Raquel asked as she unpacked a pair of dark blue-gray jogging pants and gray t-shirt. Alexander eyed it but said nothing as he shifted to one side of the bed and just sat.

"I got through most of the highlights."

"I heard they hired someone similar in appearance to you, from behind apparently, to do some shots. Though there was enough footage that they barely used him," Raquel said as she retrieved a pair of blue briefs. She walked around the bed to stand in front of Alexander, "Or would you have preferred some tighty whites?"

Alexander slid out of his hospital gown and tossed it to the bed as he reached for the shirt on the bed he felt Raquel eyes on him. "What are we doing Thames?"

"Life's a game," she answered. Alexander knew well enough that was her response.

"Was Emory still coming to fill me in?"

She shook her head and Alexander loved watching the way her sleek bob moved. There was a feeling that was still associated with the gesture, something deep that echoed but it was not the same. Maybe this had been the thing he hadn't wanted to admit. The thing the reality show had brought out of him. Things had changed yet some part of him still clung to the past. Afraid.

"Cassandra seems..." Alexander started before Raquel interrupted.

"You mean Xandra? I doubt she's coming back."

"No, not her-"

"Cashmere?"

"That's not her name is it?" Alexander paused as his head ran through the recent binge he'd done of the online soap opera. Even though it was a reality web show it reminded him of days gone past watching "Guiding Light" at his grandma's house which felt more akin to what he was involved in.

"You really did hit your head hard. And still nothing, right? No reason as to why you'd left?"

"No clue," Alexander shrugged as they cruised along the highway and the ocean greeted him back. It really was a mystery. Those that saw him said he'd been on set prepared to film and the next he was gone, having left the property but not getting very far before the accident occurred.

Alexander sighed. It was frustrating but not for the reasons one might suspect. He looked out the window and was instantly swept away instead.

"It really is beautiful here," he said.

"You mean you're finally willing to admit to me that Tré Jolla is beautiful and leaving Maryland was good. Despite the fact you're accident prone. First the cyclist incident years ago, now this."

Alexander smirked but hadn't said anything. Raquel placed a hand on his knee. The two didn't speak the rest of the way.

The videos haven't done this place justice, Alexander thought as they pulled toward the gated property. The path wound and snaked upward until finally he heard the gravel as the car approached the main entrance.

"Home sweet temporary home," Raquel declared as she threw the car in park and looked over to Alexander.

Alexander for his part was staring at the enormous mansion. One part hoped being here might stir something in the mental cogs of his foggy brain, as if seeing it would be the headlight breaking through but no such flood of memory occurred. A few people exited, faces he hadn't recognized or at least none he'd seen from the episodes.

"Still can't believe you didn't take the out."

Alexander shrugged, "She offered but I don't think she really hoped for that outcome."

"Still..."

Alexander opened his door and walked to the trunk to retrieve his duffel bag when a series of shouts caught his attention. He turned to Raquel, she'd stepped out the car and hung near the driver side. Her face equally confused.

"Never a dull moment here," she smiled just as Alexander closed the trunk.

A door slammed. As he looked up, he watched as a woman descended the steps, her head down. She hadn't looked up, but his eyes followed her until finally she did.

Just as he had done earlier, a part of him hoped for something to be triggered, for the flood of memories to hit but that wasn't what moved. Had his heart missed a beat?

They stared at teach other and Alexander, suddenly felt foolish, smiled as he tossed his bag onto his shoulder and made several steps toward her. One of the show's producers, Emory, had just came to the door, a cameraman behind him as he paused. Alexander noticed Emory looked to him then to the one Raquel called Cashmere. The name still hadn't felt right to Alexander but he'd abandoned the thought once already.

It seemed everyone stood still. It was probably just seconds. The camera's caught everything.

Are they recording now? Alexander wondered but dismissed it as he made his way to one very still Cashmere.

He extended his hand to her with a smile, "Hello Cass," he said, noting how naturally it came. This name at least felt closer to something and had been depicted as such in the letter. The words from it found him again.

Sometimes I wish we could just be strangers again...

His eyes registered hers- one moment something was reflected in those brown eyes and by the next it was gone. He watched her blink, her eyes looked down to his hand before she walked away and brushed past him.

He turned to watch her. She was walking down the gravel path, toward one of the other buildings.

Alexander found himself pulled to follow just as a hand grabbed his shoulder.

"Ash is in the kitchen. Rick wants to do a special interview with you, given the memory loss. Jaz will get you caught up with what we're doing moving forward."

"Will she be okay?"

Emory tilted his head, "Do you remember- anything?"

Alexander heard the real question. *Do you remember her?*

And the truth was he hadn't. Raquel walked over and Emory eyes met hers. Alexander hadn't missed the exchange.

"Nothing yet," he answered with a smile. For a quick moment his eyes went back in the direction Cashmere had disappeared off to.

Closet a voice in his mind said.

"Okay, I'll catch up with you later. Raquel, just one second okay?"

Emory rushed off and a camera followed behind. Alexander had already forgotten about them. Another person stood near, the camera angled at him and Raquel.

"This is going to be weird."

Raquel laughed, "You had an out," she reached up and gave him a hug. "Call if you need anything. Even if it's just to talk again or if you want to pick my mind about the gap of time missing."

"Sure, thanks."

As Alexander walked off his head was still caught in a moment. Still stuck on Cashmere. Like a stinger removed, his body felt the penetration still, reverberating in every place except the one that mattered.

Chapter 16

Cashmere

Cashmere knew better to ask. Never should one question how the day could get worse because it was like a request to the universe and their response- hold my beer.

Her hair cascaded down she quickly gathered it into her signature haphazard bun. And just as quickly pulled it back out. A moment later it was in the bun once again. She closed her eyes as her head hit the wall. She stood hidden away from the eyes, the people, she knew were still out front.

It wasn't this that had Cashmere putting her hand to her face, the pressure on her eyes to just stop, to just- not right now- she couldn't handle it...

And yet she couldn't help the memory as it assaulted her repeatedly. Seeing him had been like magic. Was it only three days ago before everything had changed? That the world stopped and threw a wrench in for good measure.

His smile was there every time as his eyes registered nothing. "Hello stranger" they said.

She shouldn't have felt so sad but it hadn't stopped her heart from crumpling, from her legs growing weak as she leaned against the side and wondered if maybe this was for the best after all.

He'd held out his hand. He looked at her and that spark, was it just her imagination or was there a tiny flicker? If only for a moment. Without a doubt she knew then what'd she known for some time. Her feelings for Alexander ran deep and everything else was just noise, just distraction, just a girl clinging to anything or anyone while yearning for a chance at authenticity.

It seemed no time at all had passed when Emory found her.

It was a warm day, the breeze rolled past them both, it carried the scent of lilacs and lavender. That was one good thing to look forward to.

"Would you at least give it some thought," Emory sighed. He'd been talking, a continuance of earlier but Cashmere had mentally tapped out. Her body and mind were still recoiling from an absence. Her spirit aching from a hurt her lips would not put into her words. Maybe the denial, the refusal to accept the truth made the hurt that much more.

"This is it," she said. Emory was talking. He'd said something. She wasn't sure. Had it been about the visit from Trevor Colton earlier? That had gone swell. He was expected to still host the delayed charity event that she was still to participate in despite the glaring fact she was no longer an ex-contestant.

"Do you want to take the car?"

Another breeze came through and she closed her eyes. She shook her head.

"Art?"

A weight filled her. So much had happened in just a matter of days. How had she gone from multiple love prospects to none again? The universe was truly plotting against her.

"Despite what you think I didn't want you voted back on but I'm also not mad that it happened. You need this Cashmere."

"What? For the 'exposure'? Emory this isn't what I need. I'm..."

Words evaporated. She pushed herself against the side and turned to Emory. She looked at him and in a blink saw the many facets of him, the versions of himself he had yet to reconcile with.

"I'm going to grab an uber."

● ● ●

"That's silly, just use my car."

She shook her head. She hadn't said the words and wouldn't allow them past her internal filter; but she suspected that Emory would soon learn that Cashmere had reached that place. That place where she no longer wanted to depend on him. That crazy gray area where friendships either thrived or died on the vine.

This was what defeat looked like Cashmere noted as she placed her bags on the bed. There'd been enough eliminations and plenty from her mouth that she was allowed to crash in one of the side buildings. It was one of the few places that hadn't been completed and was more shell than living space when compared to the rest of the property.

As she plopped down on the twin matTréss, dust kicking up in its place, at least she hoped it was dust she reached for her phone. The evening grew cooler and she was due to attend the reading in preparation for tomorrow night but part of her was still fighting, even if only a tiny bit.

> Walla walla bing bang

Ooo eee, ooo ah ah

> Ching chang

> Hey there

Hey... change your mind?

As she sat her phone buzzed with an incoming call. Emory. She pressed decline but had no an answer still. This was what Cashmere had been doing, staring at the plain ceiling when a commotion outside startled her. Somehow, she knew that as she swung the door open she'd find him on the other side of it.

"Hi," Alexander said. "I believe I'm lost."

"And unfortunately, you haven't been found."

"Ouch, that might have stung if I only had a brain."

Cashmere felt the twitch of a smirk that wanted to take shape but she fought it off, "No you have a brain. It's the lack of a memory."

"Not a fan of the Wizard of Oz, I take it?"

Cashmere leaned against the frame, crossing her arm across her pink long sleeve pajama top. "You're not lost."

"I am. I was. I-"

"Hiding. What we call this is hiding."

Alexander sighed. "How are you able to get out of this?"

"I'm not officially back yet."

"I see. So what you're telling me is I need to pull out the amnesia card more often. I see how this works."

Cashmere shook her head, "You should get back."

"Why? So they don't come here and we both go down."

"See, I knew you had a brain," she smiled as she began to close the door but Alexander reached out a hand.

"I'm sorry," he said.

She paused. She hadn't put any additional pressure on the door but her head came to rest on it. How could two words ricochet so swiftly?

"It's not your fault you don't remember."

"You were important to him, to me... I'm not sure... I'd like to talk more maybe it might help. Maybe we can get together sometime tomorrow and I could-"

"Poop debris," Cashmere said.

"What?"

"Poop debris," she repeated and the words threw Alexander off enough that she was able to close the door the rest of the way.

She waited a spell by the door. She knew he was still out there. Eventually he would give up and walk away. It was what was for the best after all. It's what they both would do when the time came. There really wasn't any other way this could end she knew.

She wasn't sure when he left, only that he had, and by the time she returned to the bed and retrieved her phone the only real answer wasn't one she had liked at all, but she sent it anyway.

> I never stop.

Chapter 17

Alexander

He hadn't meant to stare but there he was staring unbeknownst to her through the reflection of a painting. The paper in front of him, a pastry, and tea, none of which he'd recently touched.

He'd be lying if he hadn't admitted there was a morbid interest as to what it was about her. Time and time again he reminded himself it more about the mystery than it was about her truly. The mystery of the person he'd become, the type of person whose heart no longer solely belonged to one Raquel Thames: Not even she had ever made him wish to be strangers. So, what was it, he wondered as she watched her deliberately haul away all of the oranges from the fruit basket. There hadn't been many but it still seemed odd. Moments later he understood why.

"Where are the oranges?" Porchia asked as she strolled into the kitchen with a charcoal facial mask on and a towel wrapped around her head. A cameraman attached to her. "Morning Alexander."

He nodded his greeting with a toast of his tea as he resumed reading the paper with a smirk on his face. Never a dull moment indeed.

By afternoon Alexander had his very own cameraman attached to him but cameraman wasn't entirely accurate, more like a person that followed around with a phone in their hand. Phonester? Phoneman? Or PhonePerson? From binging the show he knew that the format sometimes went for a more traditional feel at times and at others it was intentionally chaotic with the screen bouncing from someone running toward the action wishing for a breath. At least that was Alexander thought they might be wishing for.

Alexander was having a private outing with Millenia. Of all the girls what stood out the most had been her height. She was either at the same height or maybe just slightly taller.

"I have two cats – Ruby and Rose. Named after someone I admire," she blushed. Alexander smiled in response as they made their way through the garden's maze. "I've been through here several times. You won't get lost with me."

"That's good to know."

"I think I should warn you about some of the other girls left."

"Oh," generally surprised Alexander hadn't looked up. It was curious and had seemingly come from out of nowhere.

"Yeah," Millenia said she leaned over to whisper to him? Or had it been an intended kiss? "Wow."

Alexander stopped.

"You really aren't you anymore. Before if I'd said something like that you'd shrug it off. You know I like you right?"

Alexander couldn't keep up and probably shouldn't have missed last night, maybe there was a game plan for this interaction? His head was about to explode.

An hour later he was hiding once again. He was due to chat with Daisy and Qamar. There was an accelerated elimination process under way and he needed to have time with all the girls, as much as possible, at every chance.

He'd taken a page out of Cashmere's book when he'd offered his Phoner, his latest attempt at the title, something to drink. About a half hour later he was without his shadow and they were occupying whatever bathroom would have them.

Alexander had been walking around the property when he stumbled upon one Cashmere. Her back was to him and she appeared to be reaching for a box on one the outside storage areas. She was wearing a yellow jumper, which highlighted her brown skin. Her hair was down.

She was standing on her toes as she reached. While there was nothing immediately sexy about the action, Alexander's body responded as he watched her, drawn to her and before he realized it he was standing beside her, grabbing the box. He held it out for her and her eyes met his.

"You could've got it, I know."

Her eyes twitched and a frown took shape before she smiled. "I guess in some ways you're still you."

"I'm still me," he confirmed as he felt her hand near his. She pulled the box toward her and he moved closer.

"I got it."

"Why does it feel like you're avoiding me?"

She laughed. An obnoxious, over the top laugh, and Alexander turned around expecting to see his Phonester had returned but it was just the two of them as far as he knew.

"I want to know..."

"Know why I'm avoiding you? Don't worry. I'm an equal opportunity avoider, it's the entire thing."

"No, I want to understand what it was that we had, I mean, I know for you this is odd or has to feel strange. But for me there's a part of me I barely know. And that person..."

"Has feelings for me," she finished. Alexander was thankful for her choice of words for whatever reason, he knew she'd intentionally avoided the 'L' word. "Shouldn't you be getting ready for the trivia event later today? Remember one 'lucky' girl gets to be on your arm tonight for the charity event."

Cashmere pulled the box from Alexander and began to walk away. He reached out for her and her skin blazed. It was hot to the touch. Or had it been him?

"Are you okay?"

"Poop debris."

"What?"

"Fine. It's fine. I'm fine, just nothing…" she said as she walked away. But Alexander seen her face, noticed her reaction. She'd felt something and whatever it was, still pained her.

Chapter 18

Two Years Earlier

"I'm not stupid," she said stepping over to his solid oak wardrobe to fetch some earrings she kept stored there. "I know you're going to work while I'm gone. I don't blame you, in fact I wouldn't be surprised if there was a work email already up."

Alexander said nothing, his face impassive as she walked over to the dresser. She watched him from the mirror as she decorated her ear with pearl studs. She was dressed in a simple black pencil skirt and burgundy ruffled top. She opted to leave her blazer hanging. Her hair was pulled into a clip but she let it come down in one swoop. She swept through it quickly before she walked over to his bedside.

"I know you," she said. He nodded and the two stared at each other.

"I'll start," she said, "I don't know. That scare did something to me and an idea shifted, it shifted before then but now I don't know. I think I might have already lost you."

"Raquel, we talked about this, it's no need to think about that just before you leave. I only intended to be honest with you."

"I know. And I appreciate that you were even after learning I was your blind date but I can't let it go and that's why I don't know. I know it was my idea. But now that I've been proven right it's not the best feeling."

"We can still try for idea. I'm not opposed to that." She shook her head, "That's the thing. Who are you doing it for at that point Alexander? Or we just holding onto something because it's easier rather than letting go?"

Alexander sighed. Raquel was one ball of confusion at times and he understood there were reasons for her plans but sometimes she got lost in the point. Especially this, she was too in her head for her own good. "It doesn't matter. I've already told them I'll do it. So I guess that just means we're on break a little while longer right?"

"They called you back," Raquel asked before remembering, "When did you call them?"

"Doesn't matter, and it's nothing official anyway seems like a couple people that were originally involved have dropped out so it might not even happen and then where will that leave us?"

Raquel hadn't answered but she smiled, "Looks like I'm rubbing off on you in all the right ways though."

He laughed, "Not sure when I became the more decisive or direct one but it's not a bad feeling."

She walked over to the bed and pressed a kiss onto his forehead, her lips hesitant as she dropped one on his cheeks and lingered before she rose, "If you're going to work keep it light. You're not as young as you think you are."

"I'm as young as I feel," Alexander said as he sat his laptop to the side and made a motion to stand. Despite the incredible height difference there was a sureness in the grace that Raquel invoked. He gave her a hug, a friend type hug, and immediately recognized the weirdness of it. She sighed and it was though they knew the answer.

"I'll be back in a few days," she said, the first to pull away, always the first and grabbed a few things before she left. Alexander considered following her out. He was only in his boxers, his face unshaven, but going after her with nothing wouldn't help. It'd only reinforce what she knew. What he knew.

What both of them denied that again they were too afraid to let go. Before Alexander could get caught in the waves of his own turbulent mind his phone rang reminding him he had work to do.

"This is Alexander," he answered as he opened his walk in closet and stared at his armor, he was ready to take on the day rather it was ready for him or not. He was coming.

Alexander exited his apartment building and standing outside was a shiny black town car. Outside it stood a driver holding a sign with Alexander's name on it. He knew it was Raquel's doing and if this gave her peace of mind he wouldn't argue. The driver was already opening the door as Alexander stepped to the car preparing to step in when at the corner stood a person in a bee costume to advertise for the new "Honey Bar" dessert shop that had just opened.

There was something about seeing the costume that triggered the memory of the woman that'd brushed past him a week ago. He shook the image from his head and stepped into the car. He tried not to think about her and focus on the day ahead instead- the contracts that needed to be saved, the outstanding web design negotiations, hell the fact he'd be out an assistant soon and missed the interview for some already- he'd at least be able to be involved with a couple interviews today- there was so much to do. And so little time.

Alexander thought he'd ridden himself of the bumblebee woman. His head leaned against the tanned window and closed his eyes for a moment. When he reopened them they'd stopped, having arrived to the building but that wasn't drew his attention it was the bee on the other side of his window and the girl that dashed across the intersection but stopped when her scarf got caught in the wind.. The driver stepped out the vehicle and opened the door, "Apologies for not dropping you off directly in front of the building. Looks like they have some sidewalk construction going on."

Alexander watched as the woman ran back for her scarf and was forced to wait. He absently nodded to the driver, "Thank you," he said handing the man a tip. Alexander reached for his briefcase and made a direct line to the intersection where the woman stood. He was almost sure, positive really, that this was no coincidence. True to form she hadn't waited for the crosswalk, she saw a break and took it. She darted across the street before he'd had a chance to make it to her.

Alexander wasn't quite suffering from PTSD but he was a bit cautious in crossing the street, waiting for the signal to cross and checking / re-checking for any cyclist Treating the streets as their personal tour de France race. He waited what felt like an eternity, the sensation of déjà vu as he watched her enter the same building he planned on. When finally his chance came he checked behind, side to side, and made a dash across the seat avoiding the treacherous jagged concrete and rubble which he technically shouldn't be crossing over but he noted how she paid no mind to the signage either. He was anxious to follow her move.

He paused to take note of the large glass building that was only ten floors tall, but was still nice to admire on a sunny day such as it was. As Alexander stared up at the building, his eyes closed and he remembered a thought he'd had not even a year ago *Why do we settle for misery?*

It was a difficult to examine when on the outside he had a good job, a beautiful fiancé, his start up was going strong and he was very notably at the top of his game. Furthermore he was appreciative of what he had but there had been moments, days, he couldn't explain when a deep depression washed over him and suddenly he realized that of everything he possessed he really hadn't wanted all of it. In fact when Alexander closed his eyes he imagined himself relaxed, floating in water, swayed by whichever direction it took him in. And when he wasn't lost to the water he was on his small plot of land sitting in a lawn chair reading a book while he cooked some fish he might've caught that day. In truth there were two Alexander's. The one that was plugged in and the one that desired to be off the grid.

Today was the day though. He sighed as he entered the sleek building and went to the reception to talk to Sue. Who jumped up immediately causing her triangular glasses to come askew.

"OMG! I was so worried," she said, swooping him into a large bear hug. Her tiny frame even might have lifted him off the ground a bit.

"Whoa, I'm not dead," Alexander squeezed out.

"No, just barely," she said coming away from him with a pissed off frown, "You of all people should be more careful. "

"I'm cautious as they come. And I adhered to the traffic signals. I can't help it if there are Lance Armstrong wanna be's cycling all over."

"I doubt they want to be Lance Armstrong," Sue corrected as she adjusted her glasses and her flower power dress, "Too much today," she asked.

"Just right for you," Alexander answered and Sue beamed. Her gap most prominent was one of the things Alexander looked for to know he was getting a true Sue smile because often times she faked it. "Where's Lynn?"

Sue shoulders dropped, "She tried to wait," she started and Alexander nodded.

"So she got the job in the Chicago market then?"

Sue nodded her face downcast. Out of everyone Alexander was sure she'd feel her absence the most. "Yeah, Grant is working with HR to get the job filled soon and we're an intern short too."

"Dropping like flies around here," Alexander smiled.

"And that's why there was so much panic when Raquel said you'd be out for a month at least, no one really, I mean there wasn't anyone speaking," Sue stumbled and Alexander put a finger to her lips.

"If anyone complained I know it wasn't you," Alexander offered when he remembered, "The Bee, I mean, hey there was a young woman that came in just before I did. Do you happen to know where she went?"

Sue shook her head, "Did she drop something?"

"No, just, I think I might know her but wasn't sure," Alexander said, it was a partial truth but alas he realized it was possible that it wasn't the same girl. What were the chances he'd run into her again anyway? In a city this size how many women were out there that had the same wavy hair strolling around. For a moment there was excitement pumping through Alexander's dormant veins, there was an idea that maybe-

"Your first appointment is ready for you in the Mercedes conference room."

Alexander smiled, feeling the prickle of his stubble, he left it there preferring it rather than a clean shaven face today. "Thanks Sue." Alexander was off toward the bank of elevators and pressed the call button. It only took a moment to arrive, there was a girl there, looking down at her phone suddenly realizing she hadn't moved. She looked up then and her mouth opened partially. Her brown-blonde hair came down in waves. She was paused from the text she'd been typing.

"Hi," she said.

The door started to close and they both reached out toward the same elevator door. Alexander stepped in. Immediately drawn to the girl that he was sure he'd never seen in the building before. She was dressed way too nice. He stood in the elevator facing her. He was only slightly aware of the door closing.

"What floor," he asked.

She took a deep breath and her eyes closed. She winced before she shook the thought from her head, "Eight please," she said as she opened her eyes, returning her gaze. "Sorry, I just got hit with a wave of déjà vu."

Alexander smiled. He was sure. He turned to hit 8, for them both, just as the elevator dinged again and someone else stepped on to Alexander's dismay.

"The old lady let you out after all," Grant said as he clasped Alexander's shoulder. Grant stood at the same height as Alexander, both towering over 6'3, though Grant often argued there was a half mark creeping toward a full inch. No one argued with him. When you were the boss people just accepted and talked about how delusional you were behind your back. Though it hadn't been the case with Grant since he welcomed criticism. He preferred being in the know.

Grant snuck a peak at the woman occupying the elevator with him and Alexander. Grant's brow rose appreciatively as he pressed the button for the sixth floor, "You won't mind a quick detour now mate? Or were you with-" Grant started for the first time considering that maybe Alexander was already occupied.

The woman shook her head just as Alexander answered, "No we just happened to be going in the same direction."

"Great, then you won't mind an ol bugger for snatching you away to talk logistics and the amount of business we've lost in your absence," Grant said jokingly. But there was no joke in the amount of money for contracts that they no longer had. Alexander just hoped he was able to leverage and note that at least the ones he'd been done with before being hit were solid. There was nothing that could be done for those in early talks. Alexander rolled his eyes and dreaded the inevitable conversation. He had hoped he'd have at least a couple hours in before he had to worry about this part. But more than that he hoped he'd had a moment alone with the girl dressed in the black pants and yellow blouse.

He wished for an audience with the bumble bee.

Cashmere was early. She had no doubt she'd arrive on time and the Crown Glass building was hard to miss in general.

But she knew from having interviewed in the past that it was best to get there early since the set up for each floor tended to be different with the exception of the restrooms. Those tended to align pretty evenly from floor to floor.

That was why she rushed to head to the lower level. Although Cashmere hadn't eaten yet, there was definitely a disturbance in the force that was her stomach. Having been to the building before she knew there would be no one in the basement bathroom. She couldn't make it there quick enough before her body ripped out whatever hadn't properly settled in her body. Then again, she'd gone a good number of hours without eating and it could be her body flushing any toxins. She wouldn't tell Emory but it was probably a good reason why she should eat. She'd remember that for her next interview.

Cashmere pushed the call button and started to fidget with her hair when she suddenly remembered she had no idea which floor she needed to go to. Had she read 6 or 8? She pulled out her phone from her cross-shoulder purse. Awaiting her were several new voicemails, two from Emory, one from Unknown, and another from Dallas. Her eyebrow arched. Dallas never called her.

There were also several texts but instead of looking through those first she checked her email for the message that verified her interview for today. 8th floor she noted just as the elevator began to move. Cashmere reached to press the 8th floor at the same time she opened a text from Emory-

> Okay chick. Listen you've been deemed a bit of a shit starter. You're not returning calls/

> Evan's having a panic attack. Wifey begged that you call back as the band is in jeopardy of missing out on a big thing. Don't ask what the big thing is.

If I were involved, I could tell you with absolute clarity what the big THING was ☺

Cashmere rolled her eyes as she continued to read.

Also did you listen to my voicemail about the gig? You didn't agree right? CALL ME BACK. Also GOOD LUCK. I hope you don't get it so we can work together again.
Love you lady.

Cashmere started to fire off a text.

First of all Em, I fully planned on calling them back. I just didn't have the mental energy for more disappointment right before a meeting. If they call you again let them know I'll call back once I get a chance.

But that was a lie, sort of. Cashmere was still hurt if she was willing to admit to it and to talk to any of them so soon was opening herself to a flesh wound where the salt still burned.

I'm not your maid. You tell them. In fact. I'm not playing go between anymore

Cashmere shook her and sighed as she began her 'begging' text before she deleted it. She was just about to type a more proper beg when the elevator chimed. She'd reached the 8th floor awfully quick, she thought, but when Cashmere looked up she was greeted by the most handsome creature she'd seen all day. He was older definitely, there were gray flicks in his beard, his sideburns, and his tousled brown hair. But it was the haunting nature of his gray eyes that trapped her.

And then the door began to close. She would lose the sight. She would no longer see him and she wasn't ready for it to be over. Not yet. She reached out to the door just as he did. Their hands brushed each other and the quick motion moved the air. Something tickled her nose faintly but then he stepped in and the scent hit her with a full force.

The scent sent her reeling. She nearly dropped her phone because she knew this fragrance. Her body sighed in a relieved exhale. Everything felt alive and when she opened her eyes there was an undeniable heat she could not ignore. There were many things that Cashmere could ignore but the scent of a man, a strong male scent, awakened her in ways that teetered toward animalistic in nature. She wanted more.

Was it her imagination? He moved in closer as if he'd heard her thoughts, knew what she wanted, and was willing to give it to her. The magnetism weighted them both. "Hi" she squeaked out. Then he spoke. He said something she should reply to. Perhaps the floor. "Eight please," she answered. And Cashmere felt stupid. She probably looked it too. She apologized before it slipped her mind and her brains turned to mush again from just the sight of him. She hated she was so affected and he seemed perfectly calm, cool; his shit was clearly together, unlike hers.

Then another guy stepped on. Cashmere withdrew, shrinking to the corner as the guy flicked a look in her direction. She tried not to listen to them until he seemed to infer something more. Cashmere was quick to correct him and didn't need to say much else. The two launched into a conversation regarding some business they needed to recover. Some conversation her presence was not needed for. She shrank into her corner of the elevator hoping to be forgotten. Hoping her slip a thing destined for the past.

A voice in Cashmere's head advised her to listen to their conversation but she didn't want to. She was still suffocating from her reaction to the man's scent. There was something about the severity of his face, the sharpness of his eyes as if he we were seeing everything in just one moment. She'd given him a nickname. Nicknames tended to be good since it meant there was vested interest on Cashmere's part. The elevator didn't stop until they reached the sixth floor. And the two men exited. He hadn't turned back around. The man with his intoxicating cologne stepped away, the elevator doors closed and she leaned her head back still enraptured with the man she'd dubbed 'The Hawk'. He had a strict vibe about him, the idea of him suited... 'PD' she decided as the elevator dinged again and she stepped off toward an interview, hot and bothered for all the wrong reasons.

Chapter 19

Cashmere

The weather was perfect. Easily in the 70's, flirting with the 80's, with a steady breeze that kept you feeling just right. Cashmere closed her eyes in thought. There was something beautifully still about the moment. Surrounded by others but isolated. Alone in a room filled with people came to mind. Except they were seated outside. To her right Haruka stifled a cough.

"Truth or dare," Cashmere whispered to Haruka.

"Truth."

Cashmere nodded. They were all seated at one long table in the backyard. Rick was getting a touch up on his makeup. While another assistant read off the rest of the day's itinerary for the hundredth time. It was a long afternoon.

"Did Sakura really do it?"

Haruka's eyes widened. "Dare."

Cashmere raised a brow and considered if she ought to say something when a scream interrupted her thoughts.

"This is ridiculous! I can't have this brand of water. Is it too much to ask to stock brands with a pH greater than 11, 10 minimum? Please and thank you."

Cashmere wasn't sure if she was more shocked that the scream was over water or Porchia's abrupt lack of manners. Someone must've complained, someone that mattered. Cashmere snuck a glance at Alexander, for his part, he was equally perplexed.

"I dare you to go give Rick some tongue."

Haruka frowned.

"Fine, how about Alexander?" Cashmere wasn't surprised by the frown that swallowed Haruka's feature further. It'd be different had she challenged Sakura, who was in love with Alexander.

"Cashmere, there's not much time left," Haruka said.

"Exactly."

"What are you planning?"

"There's a double elimination tonight."

"Yes, I know. We're getting close to the final three."

"Don't you want to be one of them, I mean, I'm sorry, wouldn't Sakura like to be involved rather than be part of the double elimination tonight? They've already got your number given Sakura."

Hakura looked at Cashmere, pity in her face, and Cashmere looked away. She hadn't wanted it. The last several days had been difficult as she avoided Alexander. Being the contestant voted back on by the fans had given her some slack but it didn't get her out of everything. It certainly hadn't give her a quick re-exit.

And she wanted to be out. She could no longer stand being around an amnesiac Alexander and pretend she was alright. It'd been over a week since she'd really spoken to anyone from MAAD Maxi, who were gearing up for a multi city tour on the east coast. Initially, Cashmere had turned it down, hoping to find another gig in the band's absence but more and more she thought 'why not'.

Plus nothing was going to happen with Art. Their conversation hours later, after he'd left her place and pre-Alexander's freak accident he'd called to apologize for his behavior. Cashmere hadn't poked any further since she'd made up her own mind. So she still wasn't sure what it was that gave him second thoughts. And it wasn't meant for her to know she decided.

It was the classic tale of how a girl went from a non-existent dating life to prospects then back to cobwebs once again. In the time Cashmere's mind had wandered she watched as Haruka made her way to one unknowing host and took hold of his head, blocking the surrounding makeup artist and went in for the kill.

All eyes were on the spectacle and Cashmere made her escape. At least she thought all eyes had been watching...

Cashmere went to their closet which wasn't far from her living space. The utility closet was as it had been before but this time she easily located the light and looked around. She grabbed a crate and made it into a makeshift seat.

The show was winding down. Emory was away more often than usual but it worked out for her. She was sure he was lining up his next project. Jazmine seemed to enjoy the freedom and calling all the shots. It suited her. She thrived in the environment. Cashmere could get behind that. This had been one of the factors for minimizing her pranks against Porchia who was still a tyrant.

There was just the charity event tomorrow that she was still attached to. She was sure Porchia would be on Alexander's arm. After tonight's double elimination there would only be three girls left. How the time had sped by...

Cashmere wasn't sure why she'd come here. She shook her head but a tear fell. She knew even if she hadn't wanted to be honest with herself.

This pain, the loneliness wasn't just the result of a lost memory. It was rooted in something much deeper, a hurt and hunger for a sort of love that was rooted in a past she kept her mind occupied from pursuing. This was her dirty secret. Her truth.

But it still hadn't kept the tears at bay. Because acknowledging doesn't stop the truth from hurting. It only casts a light on the imperfection.

"Gotta let go," she whispered to herself. She took a deep breath and as she turned around the door handle moved.

Alexander stood in the doorway. His eyes took her in before meeting hers.

"Poop debris," he said.

Cashmere sucked in an audible breath. Her hand clutched her chest as she rushed over to him and wrapped her arms around his body. He instantly held her.

"You remembered."

It wasn't a question.

It was a release.

She pulled back, tears soaked the front of his shirt and she tilted her head to him, his eyes on hers as she felt his hand dig into her hip. There was not a space between them.

"You remember," she repeated.

Chapter 20

Two Years Earlier

Alexander could still feel her. Just sharing the same space, the small confines of the elevator had his mind launching into places that were not appropriate for the afternoon and most definitely not work friendly. He half listened to Grant. Alexander wondered what might have brought the woman here. She was going to the same floor as his office. Was it possible she was one of the candidates that would be interviewed today?

The idea both excited Alexander and made him nervous. There was no way he could handle seeing her every day. He craved the possibility of it already. How was it even conceivable to be so drawn to someone you'd barely shared a word with? He wanted to know more. He had to know more and the longer Grant delayed him the less of a chance he'd have the opportunity to do so.

"So you think you can fix that at least?" Grant asked standing opposite Alexander. Grant's office had one of the best views. True to form his office was surrounded in glass, glass desk, hardwood floors that had randomly placed squares of opaque glass that illuminated if Grant chose to have them on. They could even light to the beat of music. Grant reserved that for special occasions. Alexander had yet to determine what type of occasions but he'd once noticed them on early one morning when he'd stopped by. Grant gave nothing away, except a slight smile before shifting it off.

"Alexander," Grant repeated, his head cocked to the side as he turned away from the view and pulled his rolling chair out in order to take a seat.

"Sorry, which one?" Alexander said as he shook the spell from his mind.

"You weren't paying attention were you? Still thinking about Lady Luscious from the elevator, huh? I didn't realize you had an appreciation for handles."

Alexander frowned.

"No worries mate, I do too. The meatier the better."

Alexander frowned more. "Grant, promise me to not ever say that aloud again."

Grant shrugged obviously not fazed by the HR reprimand that could come down, "Too bad we're tied down, huh?"

Alexander hitched his pants up and took a seat in one of the two chairs that were placed in front of Grant's large glass desk. "If I remember correctly only one of us is legally married."

Grant shrugged, "Semantics, you and Ray are practically married just short of the formality. I'm surprised she let you out. Did she mention the nasty spat we had on your behalf? It felt like two starved dogs fighting over a piece of rubbish meat, that's you mate."

"I was waiting for the moment you mentioned the superior being that tossed out the rubbish meat, I inferred that might be me."

Grant barked a laughter, tears flooded his eyes. It was times like these that Alexander could reflect on just how young at heart Grant was even though he was the kind of guy that adopted 'there's no such thing as impossible'. Grant, despite the gray that had slowly taken over the traces of glossy back hair, was constantly reinventing himself when at his age most would be trying to ensure they were on target for an early retirement. Grant hadn't thought that way, in fact he believed to do so was put a nail into his coffin. "Live brother, live," he'd said once to Alexander as he cupped his shoulders. At the time it resonated with Alexander in the sense that it felt so out of place, the words appeared out of thin air while they were attending a charity recognizing many of the small companies with big green initiatives.

Grant rubbed his eyes, "Well you definitely have a strong lady *friend* or whatever you two are calling yourself these days. The band," Grant said directing the conversation back to where his concern lie, "will you be able to meet with them today? Maybe just to get a brief and give the impression you'll be taking it on."

Alexander shook his head, "I promise to reach out to them but I honestly don't think I have the time today. I'm still without an assistant and have to get that taken care of before I truly get backed up."

Grant narrowed his eyes and bit his bottom lip.

"I can't even entertain it because we both know that's not where it's going to stop. I don't mind being part of the package if it gets them to give over the contract but is it necessary for me to meet with them?"

Grant nibbled at the poor bottom lip, "Carrie seems to have gotten them for the most part but they still want to sit down with you personally. I think that's just their style and frankly their paying to be in capable hands. Can't say I blame them for wanting to meet those capable hands." Grant said as he reached for his cell phone.

"Listen I have a meeting coming up soon. We'll talk before you go, since I know you'll be here late but consider this. They're open to talking with you tonight."

Grant wouldn't let it go. Alexander could tell from the posture of his body, poised like a cat ready to pounce he wouldn't back down. Alexander closed his eyes in resignation, suppressing another sigh and simply nodded. Already he was losing battles at work. Though if his battles with Raquel were any indication of his success rate he had a significant amount of failures lined up.

"I'll pencil it in," Alexander said making a notion to get up from the chair. He walked back toward the door where he'd left his laptop bag on a table adjacent to the glass wall. There was a beautiful glass vase that hadn't been there before. Alexander looked at it and noted the sunflowers present in it. Already he remembered the woman that was up on the eighth floor somewhere.

There was a budding anticipation of figuring out where she might have gone or take another look at his roster to see if any of the prospective assistant candidates could be her. Disappointment marred this thought however, Alexander was sure all the names listed were male candidates.

"Great, I'll catch you later," Grant said getting up as well, "Looks like there's a bit of a fire with the Charpin campaign and the boss needs to do some damage control."

"That's why they pay you the big bucks," Alexander said before Grant could get the words out himself. Grant always fell on making this remark whenever there was a problem. For him to be rushing out to attend a meeting, and not take the opportunity to lay into Alexander for his absence in Grant's cleverly insensitive ways, was an indicator that he had no time to dolly about.

The two exited Grant's office into a flurry of activity that hadn't been there before. Several interns rushed past, with stacks of PowerPoint bounded printouts in their hand that looked like a shuffled deck. All the cubicles here were glass as well and were only about four and a half feet to ensure you could look over directly in the eyes of your neighbor. Alexander wasn't a fan nor was Grant, however Grant didn't like the idea of walls at all. His initiative for next year intended to go more toward open spaces. Alexander just hoped his own business was strong enough by then that he might be able to finally leave. He loved his job most days, and it had served him well, but he was ready for more self-investment in the means of his own passions. And he hadn't left the legislative world just to end up in a similar break-neck setting.

At the elevator one of the interns rushed over to Grant, "They need you in the Legacy conference room."

"Can't, have a meeting I need to get to," Grant said as an elevator arrived. Alexander stepped aboard first.

"It's the board," Zion, one of the newer interns, said.

Grant mumbled something about the perks of being public and waved Alexander off. He'd started to walk away when he yelled, "Oh by the way," Alexander pressed the door open button as a devilish grin graced Grant's face. "Pass on a hi to Cashmere for me. I think she's up first."

"Who?"

"Your assistant, Lady Luscious from earlier. She's one of the interviewees today. Try to keep it contained Alexander. Women have a way of sensing these things."

Alexander was floored. He had a name. He finally had a name and it applied, it felt right for the woman he'd only called the bumble bee up until now, but then he remembered his roster. He had a list of three thirty-minute interviews, he wasn't sure he'd even get to them all and if he did, he intended to cut them to fifteen but nowhere was there a Cashmere listed.

"There's no Cashmere," Alexander said simply. The elevator was in threat of going off soon from his holding it.

Grant narrowed his eyes again, this time in thought. Zion bounced from side to side, his mouth visibly twitched despite the beard that covered it. His strapped gray pants and red shirt gave him a modern hipster Urkel look that probably also steered others away as well Alexander considered. *This is my life...*

"She's there. I spoke with all of the potential just in case you couldn't make it in."

"There's no-" Alexander began to protest, frustrated now and releasing his finger from the button.

"Watson," Grant smiled, "Amy prepares her list differently. Have fun with it mate," Grant winked and strolled off. Zion followed close behind. The elevator doors closed slowly.

The sixth floor disappeared away from him as a new reality, two short flights, awaited him.

Alexander hit the button for eight. He was late for another meeting but could be ten minutes early for his first interview with the guy he'd assumed as Watson.

He could finally meet his bumble bee.

Cashmere was still reeling. She thought of that scent knowing she'd experienced it not so long ago. She searched through her memory- clubs, coworkers, temporary gigs, even concerts for MAADD Maxi and drew a blank on where she might've come across the scent before. She was sure it was recent. It was there on her memory trying to be recovered, just at the tip of her tongue but every time she got close it evaporated. Almost as if her mind had tried to tell her 'yes you're on the correct path' but the slightest shift in thought and it went 'poof'.

Her phone buzzed, she knew it was no one other than Emory she answered it without really looking. She only noticed afterwards the caller was 'Unknown'. It was possible the interview for later on tonight was calling her back to let her know that she was no longer needed as they'd canceled, filled the role, or some other run-of-the-mill way of saying she was rejected.

"Hello, this is Cashmere," she said, inserting as much sweetness as she could into her voice.

There was a deep breath exhaled on the other end but no actual words had been uttered.

"Hi, this is Cashmere," she said this time and a voice cleared. "Hello?" She asked but when nothing came, she hung up the phone. Once she disconnected the call, she noticed several texts from Emory.

This is me not being the go between but word on the street has it the band might be breaking. WTF DID YOU DO? Been giving out that good good, huh? It was Dallas wasn't it?

Another text a few minutes later read-

Or was it Art?

The last text read-

For real chic, did you take any suspicious gigs recently? I warned you about the one. Call me back ASAP. We need to talk.

Cashmere had been walking down a short corridor upon exiting the 8th floor to a reception desk where there was large silver lettering that said "GIANT" and in black cursive lettering on the light gray wall was what Cashmere assumed was the company motto which read, "There wasn't an 'I' in GRANT, so we named it GIANT." The quote was by its founder Grant Anderson. And like it's owner it made no sense except only to him and his loyal followers.

"May I help you," the receptionist asked, his accent thick. She wondered if he might be related to the founder.

"Cashmere Watson, I have an interview today at 1:30" she said as she typed out a quick reply to Emory before he sent another text that bordered along the lines of 'do not ignore me'. Emory was liable to blow up her phone if he so chose to.

> About to interview soon. Have a gig tonight, not sure which one you're referring to. Will check vm later and give you a call afterwards
>
> xoxo CA

Cashmere thought it was clever, on her part, to sign that way and was absently smiling when she heard the receptionist mumble something along the lines of 'now I know his definition of fun'.

The receptionist with his clean-shaven globe, was a hot guy easily in his early thirties, and obviously not satisfied with his place in work. His tight light blue shirt and darker blue slacks left nothing to the imagination with how much they clung to him, Cashmere quickly noted the only thing endearing about him was the red and white polka dot bowtie that didn't appear to be a clip on and his Australian accent, even his blue eyes held no excitement. She figured it was partially due to the lackluster vibes he dished out.

"So you're late," the receptionist said, not looking at her, "Says you were supposed to start at 11:30."

Cashmere frowned, "No I had a follow up interview today."

"And you spoke to Grant directly twice now, right?"

"Well yes, but-"

He gave a contemptuous smirk, "You started at 11:30, you'll learn quick, no worries but you're behind the curve on the paperwork. Let's have you meet with Mr. Roth first and I think he has some things to go over with you then we'll worry about your Government's paper trail."

Cashmere had to remember to close her mouth and hold back her tongue. She wasn't liking the receptionist and now she was supposed to have started a job that she hadn't been given an offer for. Something was about to get it and she wasn't sure who it might be. "I haven't agreed to anything."

"Right," the reception said not looking at Cashmere at all, his head already back on the swanky silver computer monitor. He keyed in a few characters, frowned, keyed in another set, sighed and took a note. "You can have a seat in Mr. Roth's office. He's running late from another appointment but he should be in his office to walk with you shortly."

"I haven't agreed to it," Cashmere repeated again but she knew she wasn't going to deny the sudden good luck that'd befallen her. At this rate, if the money way right, she could probably forego the later gig. Though some quick cash still didn't sound too bad.

The receptionist still hadn't heard Cashmere. He simply handed her a piece of paper, gave some directions and buzzed her through the heavy frozen glass doors. On the other wide there was a flurry of contained energy. People were on phones at large desk spread nearly from one end of the room to the other. There were no walls to separate one space from the other. It was open. There were people huddled near white boards and doing an old fashioned idea sessions with colored post its. She liked that even though the building screamed tech there were some old school brainstorming to be had.

Some people smiled as Cashmere passed. Their faces were extremely friendly. Already she was considering it might not be a bad place to work at after all. She found Mr. Roth's off easily but true to the receptionist's word he wasn't there and looked like he hadn't been there for some time or he was in such a desperate need for assistance that several of his plants were dying a slow death and there were several interoffice packages sitting precariously on his desk. Cashmere straightened the pile despite it had survived not falling over at this point.

Once she was satisfied it wouldn't topple over she took a seat opposite the solid wood desk. It was a nice rich dark brown that seemed out of place with so much glass. But it hadn't been the only thing, the back wall was exposed brick with a few awards that graced it. Cashmere wondered if there might be something on the other side considering the building, from the outside, appeared to be total 360 glass view even though she hadn't walked the parameter to know if it was a fact.

Cashmere's phone buzzed with a new text from Emory, she'd seen the first line of the sentence but wasn't really looking at it as she began to google 'The GIANT building' just as the door opened from behind her and closed quickly. She shot up from her seat and turned to face the source of the noise but it wasn't that that really had her mind going. It was the scent. The familiar scent.

It was the man from earlier. He stood at the door for a moment, his eyes focused on her and their eyes locked for an indeterminate amount of time before he cleared his throat and broke the trance.

"Good morning," he said, his eyes finding hers again.

"Afternoon," she corrected.

"Right," he said leaving her eyes again to walk over to his desk where he sat his book-bag on a counter adjacent to the brick wall. His desk chair ping ponged between the two. He sat down and Cashmere followed suit. "I'm sorry, Alexander Roth," he said reaching out for her hand over the desk as he stood again.

"Cashmere Watson, pleasure to meet you."

"I assure you the pleasure is all mine," he said in a way that made their contact sizzle more than it should, the base in his voice taking on a tone that Cashmere tried to not let impact her even as she felt his grip tighten, his eyes lower, and then the phone rang. They parted quickly- she pulled her hands away, wished to stuff them and pretend she wasn't trouble at all by his presence.

Alexander tapped the intercom on his desk phone, "This is Alexander."

"Should I reschedule your 2pm appointment," the receptionist asked.

"Yes," Alexander answered quickly and hung up the phone. He hadn't waited for a reply and Cashmere was amused by it. "I trust you've met Randy,"

"I have," Cashmere said, again biting back the whip of her tongue that wanted to advise Alexander he might be in need of a new receptionist with more people skills.

"He's a bit of an asshole but he's the boss's nephew so you can speak bad of him all you like but the likelihood of his going away is about as likely as becoming a millionaire tomorrow."

"I'll take my chances," Cashmere smiled, "He also informed me I was already on the payroll but I was under the impression this was an interview today and not a welcome to the company thing."

Alexander shook his head on a small smile that made Cashmere return one, "Bit of a gambler that one. Grant knows I like to throw people head on first when I take on a new assistant and I think he was just taking the leap that you'd be a good fit based on your skill set and the fact that he's wanting me to make a bit of an outcall today to lock in a negotiation. You interested?"

Cashmere was impressed by the quickness of it all. "Don't you want to delve a bit deeper before you just offer me a job."

"I do," Alexander answered simply, his eyes locked onto Cashmere once more. Another moment passed before he asked, "I need to meet the band in another hour. We can ride over together if you don't mind."

"Is this supposed to be some sort of trial," Cashmere asked, her brow raised.

"You can call it that but I think it's a good look at seeing what you'll be getting yourself into. In fact this could be a good thing for you if you think about it. You'll get a preview before you sign on the dotted line. And I'll ensure you're compensated for your time regardless. How does that sound?"

Cashmere smiled, "Don't beat around the bush here do you?"

Alexander's eyes smiled but his lips hadn't moved. A careful stillness entered the room, the silence allowed Cashmere to become more attuned to her other senses, namely her sense of smell and that scent overcame her once more. Alexander's lips parted slightly and the motion made a soft gasp leave her own. She crossed her legs and cleared her throat.

"I think," Alexander started, a thought flitted across his mind and Cashmere watched with apt attention, "I think we've met before," he finished.

Cashmere sat straighter, "I thought something about you seemed familiar," she said without elaborating just how so.

Alexander nodded but didn't give anything further despite Cashmere's interest to know.

"Where," she asked getting straight to the point.

"So you don't remember," Alexander fake frowned and as his body slumped. "I can't believe you've forgot already."

Cashmere allowed herself a moment of guilt before Alexander gave himself away with a very visible smirk, "We haven't have we?"

"Not officially no. This is going to sound strange but I think we crossed each other's paths last week while at an intersection. You sort of rudely brushed past me unapologetically trying to get to the other side. But we were heading the same place about a week ago, *The Southern Belle.*"

Cashmere racked her mind and finally fell on the memory, the man standing at the intersection, the wind that swept the scent of his cologne her way, "I remember" she said. "I was on my way to Belle for a company happy hour." Cashmere smiled and feeling bold added, "Your cologne, it's blends well with you."

Alexander nodded and paused, "I'm afraid anything I say at this point are all grounds for HR remediation, but I'm almost tempted to not care," he leaned in whispering. His eyes were intent as they watched her. Her own gaze unwavering as well.

"Are you seeing anyone," Cashmere posed, leaning in and feeling bolder by the second. She was sure it might not be in her best interest to take the job but the male specimen opposite her seemed too much of a good offer to pass up.

Cashmere noted the flinch of Alexander at the question. He sank back into his seat, a visible frown line marred his forehead. He opened his mouth, then shut it. He did this twice before finally his mind settled on saying, "It's complicated. My ex-fiance has recently come back into my life. I had a bit of an accident last week and she's been around helping me."

"But you two aren't an item, right?"

"That's where the complication comes," he sighed. Alexander shook his head, "Best first day of a job, huh?"

"Well technically this was supposed to be an interview so it's the most fascinating one I've had today."

"How many interviews did you have today," Alexander asked suddenly curious If there was a chance that maybe, for her at least, this was still an inquiry for her part, that maybe she might go for the job after all.

"Just one other later on today," she shrugged. "So I guess your ex is still hung up on you I take it?"

"Something like that. I think she wants us to give it another try."

"And you don't," Cashmere added, hoping that might be the case.

"I think it took me sometime to see her point but it finally occurred to me she was right. And now that I finally see what she had wanted me to see all those years ago she wants us to be back on again. We've been on again, off again, over the last ten years, sometimes it feels longer than that and... I don't know why I'm telling you all of this. Most inappropriate work conversation ever."

"I can think of worse. Waaaay worse. But it's okay, I have that effect on people," Cashmere joked, "Your confessional is safe with me. I won't track down your ex-fiancé and yell 'he's not into you anymore, let it go', though I'm available for break up calls if you need some third party non-bias individual to handle it for you. You two are at least living separately right? No messy split over who gets to keep the house or the Scooby right?"

Alexander belted a deep belly laugh, "Does that come with a new life too?"

"It could."

"And how about a happy ending," Alexander joked but immediately he regretted the words. The room became charged again. Cashmere eyes locked onto Alexander eyes, then his lips, and back to his eyes again.

"Are you," Alexander said, his voice barely above a whisper but Cashmere heard and knew what he'd been asked. Cashmere shook her head

This was not a job interview. It was an interview of another kind. Two desperate souls that sought to connect.

Cashmere pictured herself, walking over to the other side of the desk, where Alexander sat, her looking down at him, wanting to take the lead but opening the door for him to take control. In the fantasies that followed she took over the majority of the time- kissing him fiercely, straddling his laps, gripping his shirt but it was the ones where he stood, imposing his height onto her and taking the lead that made her body burn with desire.

Still she sat.

As did he.

The phone rang. The moment broken.

"This is Alexander." Cashmere noted how heavy his breath appeared. She wondered, as his eyes met hers, the thoughts that had filled his mind.

• • •

There was something about the shift that struck Cashmere and without meaning to she'd licked her parched lips but the motion struck another chord for Alexander. Alexander was on the phone but Cashmere felt his attention was solely on her.

As Alexander listened, Cashmere unable to continue staring at him without riling herself she opted to check her phone where there were several text from Emory.

"I'll have to check," Alexander said to the person on the phone, "But I'm not guaranteeing. I still need to salvage a few contracts remember you were insistent about."

Grant Cashmere thought, it had to be the founder who else could totally uproot a moment when it was obvious Alexander was feeling similarly to her.

The conversation went on for another five minutes. Emory's text were more of the same. Checking to see how her interview went, curious about the gig, wanting to know what she wanted for dinner, and some other nonsensical things that could wait.

"We'll talk later," Alexander said ending the call.

"Doesn't sound like you got much in."

"With Grant it's it always tend to be a one sided conversation. Grant wants to celebrate the new additions, including you, happy hour tonight."

"I'm not a fan."

"How did I know you'd say that," Alexander smiled, "Grant might not like that."

"Does that mean I'm officially out of the job I haven't accepted but already am an employee for?"

Alexander laughed and swirled his chair around, he reached into his book bag and retrieved his wallet. "Look, I'm not going to pressure you into attending. I think you might even earn some respect for those of us who wanted to do just that when we started but ended up going. But I will say that if you go I'll attend as well seeing as your sort of my new assistant."

"Emphasis on the sort of," Cashmere said.

"Heavy emphasis on that," Alexander nodded, "might even say you're a non-assistant assistant."

Cashmere threw her head back in a laugh, "I doubt n if that can even be considered a thing"

"I think we just made a thing."

"That's it, we've declared it a thing,"

Alexander slammed his fist on his desk, "ARRIBA"

"ARRIBA, DOLCE Y GABANA," Cashmere yelled, slamming her fist down onto Alexander's desk as well.

Alexander's fist rested on the desk, his body leaned in again, "I like your level of random Watson."

"Ditto Roth."

"I think I might even hire you," Alexander said standing up and grabbing his keys.

"I think I might even say yes," Cashmere said rising.

Simultaneously they both asked, "Ready?"

They smiled, they exited Alexander's office arm to arm, fingers tingling for more. They weren't hand on hand but their bodies knew it was only a formality.

At that moment, they were in sync. They both were ready.

Chapter 21

Alexander

If things weren't awkward already they'd grown even more complicated. Keeping himself busy he attempted to not look over in Cashmere's direction whenever her laughter reached his ears. Was it real? Or was she fighting off the earlier interaction?

For his part Alexander regretted his choice of words but it had at least confirmed something he hadn't intended. The words held some meaning and Cashmere, in her own way, had hoped they would trigger something for him. They hadn't.

"Poop debris," he'd said and before the laugh in his mind could find an existence on the outside she'd rushed him. The contact was intoxicating, he closed his eyes, and even if his mind couldn't his body remembered.

"Oh so you want to be an astronaut?" Alexander heard Cashmere excitedly say to one of the kids.

There'd been a push to do something else in the community with the remaining girls. On a Sunday night there weren't too many opportunities but Ethel, who'd worked in Social Services had suggested a friend who fostered several children. Ethel, although no longer a contender, even attended and she wasn't alone Alexander noted. He wondered how many of the women involved with the show had partners they were returning to.

There was one definite couple on the show— Haruka and Millenia—who were set to be eliminated tonight. Alexander was surprised the producers hadn't attempted to use this to their advantage. The two were currently occupied by a set of twins making paper airplanes. They looked like a family.

"Cute aren't they," Ethel said as she came from behind toward Alexander. Alexander was still holding one of the toddlers who dozed off while he'd been reading. Ethel grabbed another chair and sat down. "How have you been?"

"Better but can't complain. How's life on the outside?"

Ethel laugh, "About the same minus a little bit of fifteen minutes of fame. I even have a fan page and an online petition for me to have my own show."

"Impressive."

"Humbling," Ethel said as she looked down at her hands. "But it's hard you know."

"How so?"

"There was someone I met during the filming that I haven't forgotten."

"Complications?"

Ethel gave a half-hearted laugh, "Aren't there always? It's okay but it was nice. Even if brief. There's always a reason to not do something Alexander. So much easier to judge than to work for that thing."

"Are you about to sing Lauren Hill?"

She laughed and shook her head, "I'm glad to see you still have your sense of humor. You once told me you were a 'by the books' type of guy. Had your life all figured out and thought you were happy until you weren't. You'd glimpsed something just above eye level and couldn't keep your head from the clouds after that."

"I said all that?"

Ethel stood up as the toddler stirred in Alexander's arm, "Looks like someone else is waking up."

Alexander looked down. Ethel gave a squeeze to his shoulder, "It'll be PD…"

"What?" Alexander turned to Ethel, she wore a confused expression.

"It'll be okay," she said but that hadn't been what Alexander had thought he'd heard. And again it occurred to him there was something more…

But it'd have to wait because seconds later Porchia was vomiting into a kid's Lego tub and collapsing onto the floor. Alexander turned to Cashmere who was watching as well before she rushed over to help.

Cashmere was the last to arrive to the reading that night. Porchia wouldn't be there. The lighting felt unusually bright to Alexander.

The reading had been moved to the kitchen. Unusual for crew but these were unusual times. Emory, who'd been MIA a lot recently was there. Alexander noted how Cashmere looked to him, then decided on sitting elsewhere until realized that meant being across from Alexander. She stood beside Hailey instead.

"Don't even," Hailey started.

Cashmere sighed, "For the umpteenth it wasn't me. I didn't do anything to Porchia."

Alexander noticed how Cashmere's eyes quickly flitted over to Haruka, currently Sakura, who had sat on the couch opposite him. Sakura for her part looked at Alexander and smiled. Given the situation with Porchia there was a lot in jeopardy.

"You've had it in for her since the beginning. Just admit it. You did something to her food. There was NO reason for her to suddenly get ill if something hadn't done something to ensure that."

"Hailey," Jazmine started. "We don't know anything."

"We don't? She's having an incredible reaction and from day one there's only been one person whose single handedly been the reason for that. Unless you all know something that we don't." Hailey again turned accusatory eyes to Cashmere, but Alexander observed the truth in her sentiment, and he suspected the crew knew something.

"Well, if I may interject," Rick began, "the ratings are doing quite superb and I'm sure our dear Porchia could appreciate this."

"Yeah, if she doesn't die," Hailey said as she crossed her arms. "What are you all going to do about this? This is clearly not safe and I don't feel like I'm-"

"You should leave," Sakura said.

Hailey looked at Sakura. Cashmere was dressed in her pajama's but bounced with restrained energy. Alexander tilted his head. Something in this felt familiar.

"Hailey is right."

"Why is she even still here?"

Cashmere and Hailey had spoken at the same time.

"Back-up," said Emory, Jazmine, and Rick at the same time. If things were suspicious already, they certainly seemed that way to Alexander now.

Hesitant, her eyes briefly flashed to a smiling Sakura, "Does this mean that Cashmere will be escorting Alexander tomorrow?"

"No," Sakura interjected. "Sakura was number two."

There'd been a game earlier of who would have the charity date with Alexander tomorrow evening. Alexander had noticed Cashmere hadn't even tried and Haruka had scored bonus points for her stunt.

"Technically," Emory started "it was Haruka..."

"Same, same."

"And you are off the show, the backup contingency is based on if Por-"

"It's based on online polling," Jazmine interrupted as she looked to Emory, her eyes wide. Emory nodded. Alexander sat back and observed it all. He shot a glance toward Cashmere who still looked as though she itched to be out of her skin. There were headlights, near the window which Cashmere stood, and she turned to peek out the curtains.

"I should just leave," Cashmere started, "Hailey shouldn't feel as though her life is at risk with me here... even if all my pranks have been childish at best." She rolled her eyes.

"We're looking into things," Emory started, there was a crisp tone to his voice and it was directed at Cashmere. "Alexander," he started, "we'll leave it up to you. Unless Porchia makes a solid recovery by tomorrow evening."

Cashmere looked up just as Alexander's eyes found her. He knew without a doubt.

Chapter 22

Cashmere

There was bad blood between Rick Hudson and Trevor Colton. The type she could understand as she canceled her Uber driver during an apparent service surge last night. Not that she had the cash to spare she still paid them and tipped despite not using the service. This did nothing to lift the driver's demeanor.

You can't please these damned cats Cashmere laughed remembering Ms. Devers, the resident cat lady from her block back home. It was true. She recognized anyone trying to make her happy was likely to encounter a similar reaction from her. You can't make everyone happy and it was a hard truth to accept.

Even Alexander. Who might have picked her with his eyes last night, he ultimately opted to have Hailey escort him to tonight's charity event. His reasoning, he shared, was based on the fact that she was due to be eliminated.

Just like that Cashmere's own plans evaporated. She was due to give Evan and the band an update tonight. Being in the final three meant she was still involved on the show but it also meant she had almost a week to herself. For the last three contestants Alexander was due to spend a few days with each.

Luckily it was almost over and Cashmere tried to look on the brightside. At least she got a paid trip back home. Her stomach rumbled in response.

"The stars aligned for Emory, nice weather, location, ambiance…" Qamar, one of the other contestants, said as she handed Cashmere a drink. "So just a dance?"

Cashmere was in her head as she took the glass. Still pissed about her failed plan to get the boot a second time. Tonight she wore a yellow romper with an electric blue belt and leather jacket. She noted that Qamar decided against traditional wear and looked more like she belonged with the engineer Barbie crew with her metallic pink dress.

"I bid on your 'day in the life of a vet' experience and Francesca's horror movie makeup tutorial," Cashmere answered instead.

"So, you're anticipating that no one will bid on your dance, huh?" Qamar smirked. She tilted her glass toward Alexander, "I don't care if he doesn't have his memory. You two are still itching."

"They have cream for that," Cashmere said as she placed her empty glass on the tray and grabbed a fresh glass from one of the waiters passing. "Did you hear about Porchia?"

Qamar nodded, "You're telling me they just now figured out how unstable Sakura is?"

"They know now. Haruka seems to be back in the driver seat at least. Millenia arrived this morning."

"They always knew," Qamar mumbled into her glass. "Fucking ridiculous. I bet you're glad it's almost over. You know there's a rumor..."

"I'm good. This is a rumor free zone," Cashmere started and paused for the length of a breath before she said, "Oh hell, did you notice that Trevor is hosting tonight? What is that about? I'm surprised Rick isn't here threatening to stab him with that same knife Trevor used on him."

Qamar choked on her drink, "So much drama but that's what I was getting at. Rumor is Trevor is talking to a network to host something similar. They've been paying attention to the ratings on the web, the shares, meme's, it's crazy Cashmere. Like I wouldn't be surprised..."

The world dropped out from beneath Cashmere's feet as something clicked into place. Emory's absence. Trevor's visit that day, the same day as Alexander's accident. It couldn't be related... could it? Cashmere had played around with the idea of the show's success and what could happen. Was it possible that Emory no longer needed Rick and now worked with Trevor for an even bigger project? The alcohol was kicking in for sure.

"Ladies," Ash said walking up, "does anyone need a touch up."

Cashmere downed her drink, "No thank you."

Qamar smiled, "Sure." The two walked off and Cashmere scanned the bar in search of Emory just as a couple guys approached her.

"Those don't look like dancing shoes. I hope you're able to keep up," the guy said as he smiled at Cashmere. "Would you like another drink?"

"You do realize you could bid on a date with Heather?"

The guy shrugged, "I bid on several, hoping the odds are in my favor."

Cashmere wondered if she could get to the table and outbid him without anyone noticing she was occupying a slot for her item. This wasn't as simple as she thought it was and as the minutes crept by more and more people turned up at the bar. They had to be reaching capacity. How had no one thought to make this an exclusive event?

"So are you and that girl *Porta* really not friends in real life?" They slurred.

"Well we're friends in fake world but in fantasy land we're actually lovers. It's complicated. Pardon me." Cashmere turned around to walk off and bumped right into the chest of Alexander, whose eyes weren't on her but the two guys.

"Hey," he offered as he looked down to her. Into her ear he whispered, "I thought you might need some help." The heat lingered, his mouth held, and Cashmere gripped his shoulders. His hands at her hips in turn did the same.

Cashmere's breath quickened, heat surged, was it the alcohol? Had to be.

"I can't do this," she said as she let go and walked away.

"Cassidy."

She'd thought she'd heard him say. She'd imagined she'd heard him. She imagined so much these days.

Half an hour in the bathroom hadn't been long enough. It was Qamar who'd retrieved Cashmere.

"Lucky you, you're up first. They are announcing the winning bid for your item. Trevor's called out your name a few times now."

Cashmere hadn't the energy. She nodded and got up. She caught herself in the mirror. Qamar stopped as well.

"I think I'm going to dye my hair."

As the two walked back into the crowded bar there were a few things that struck Cashmere. A scent, it was familiar, she'd brushed past it on her way toward the stage; she couldn't dedicate more thought to it. The next was Alexander and the back of the head of a woman that wasn't Hailey. Cashmere forgot to check out what Alexander had up for bid.

Lastly the bar was overflowing. Qamar carved a path for them as they attempted to get through the sea of people. She couldn't ignore how much of a hit their show was despite the many lies fed to them that it was suffering. It had always been a numbers game. The powers that be wanted more and more. And so, an image had been hand fed to them for most of the time.

"This is crazy," Qamar yelled to Cashmere.

"Aw here she is!" Trevor said into the microphone, "Our curvy vixen, Ms. Cashmere Watson!"

Trevor winked to Cashmere as he took hold of her hand so that she could step on stage.

"And we had quite the interest for a dance. With a winning bid of one thousand dollars..."

Cashmere looked over to Alexander who was still distracted but she had the impression it was for show. However, she still wondered if he had.

* * *

"Finn Jake."

The crowd erupted in applause, but Cashmere eyes narrowed. She knew that name was made up by someone who obviously liked a show she was familiar with. She half expected to see Art but as 'Finn' made their way toward the stage her mouth dropped.

"You can settle your amount with Yuna in the back," Trevor said, moving the mike away from his lips.

"Thank you, Cashmere. Talk soon, k." Trevor said as he placed a quick kiss on Cashmere's cheek and returned his attention to his index card. He began reading out the next item. Cashmere, caught in a trance followed, as something in her stirred. Once backstage she took hold of his extended hand.

"What are you doing here?"

Dallas smiled.

"Seriously," she persisted.

"Buying a dance."

"Dallas, I don't think... You shouldn't have done that."

Dallas stopped by the table where there were two attendants and Cashmere was beside herself, she still searched for words.

"Some things have changed recently. I decided to come out and meet you."

"Okay."

"The band is taking a break. Amy and Mike need the time. Dylan and I still plan to perform, under a new name."

Cashmere noted the absence of one name. Dallas was returned his credit card and given a slip to sign as Cashmere asked, "And Art?"

Dallas paused in his scribble, his body hunched over, before he finished off his signature. As he returned to his full height Cashmere noted that while he still had an effect on her it'd changed.

"I do believe I'm owed a dance."

Cashmere nodded; she held off pursuing it... for now.

When they returned from backstage and to the bar. "Want to go out on the patio?"

Cashmere gave a thumbs up.

Dallas, with Cashmere's hand in his, led the way. It seemed the crowd parted for them. Once outside Cashmere appreciated the night breeze. Tré Jolla's breezes were the best. Even better was that the patio was moderately occupied since most people were inside trying to hear if they were the winning bid.

Dallas spun Cashmere and pulled her back despite the fact they weren't on beat to the song in any sense. But that didn't stop Dallas from bringing Cashmere in closer and holding her as they swayed. She wrapped her arms around his neck.

"I owe you an apology. Art wanted to apologize too, but I begged him to hold off. So, I'm sorry."

"For…"

"A lot of things. You've always been important to us, you know that right?"

Cashmere nodded and Dallas pulled her closer, at this point they'd welded into one. Quiet descended upon them both.

As the song ended, they continued despite everything. The sounds of the people inside, the knowledge they weren't alone, and the idea cameras could be capturing this all. For Cashmere, it hadn't mattered because it was nice to just be held.

Cashmere wouldn't admit to it but she owed Dallas a favor at that moment. She might've been in the thick of her fifteen of fames, surrounded at a crowded bar but his arms secured her. Tonight, for the moment, she wasn't swallowed whole by the loneliness.

Chapter 23

Alexander

"Something wrong?"

"The band," Cashmere started, "You said the contract you had to work on was for a band right."

"Right," he confirmed a little confused by her sudden change, "You've probably heard of them before- MAADD Maxi? I was supposed to work on their site but had a bit of an accident last week and had to delay it to today."

Cashmere looked at Alexander, an expression on her face he wasn't sure of. She still smiled. She turned away.

"You ever feel like you're caught in a loop? Life repeating itself?"

The scene changed. She was standing just below the neon "Open" sign and flicking it off. She was staring out the storefront window when Alexander approached.

"You ever feel as if we're doomed to repeat it, I think maybe that's why."

"Why what?"

"Why I've always seen you. And you me. We see it in each other, we don't point fingers because there's three pointing right back." Cashmere was pacing now. Alexander stopped; his eyes followed her. "We say we're ready. We tell ourselves this beautiful lie but the first chance we get, the fear takes control. We have to break it."

Cashmere's phone buzzed and Alexander was at her side looking over her shoulder.

"Who is—?"

Cashmere smiled and reached for his cheeks, she moved in. Alexander leaned forward as she whispered. Her mouth at his ear lobe. His hands snaked around her body and as she stood there, he couldn't help but feel a sensation throughout his body. This was right. Just as his lips moved in a bell sounded.

"Are you going to get that?"

Alexander's eyes popped open as he stared at a familiar ceiling that was not room he'd recently grown accustomed to. The phone continued to ring and Alexander rolled over to mute the call. Time had become a tricky affair.

As his mind woke so did a flash forward of the last week. The auction—the last place he'd seen Cashmere—had gone well but images of her in her electric blue had been memories he clung too. At least until now. Was the dream an actual memory? If so, it'd be the first.

The doctor had said his memory could come back at any time, was it finally happening? Now that the time was approaching for him to spend with Cashmere. She was the last one he had time allotted for. Each of the final three got three days.

The night of auction had also been Hailey's last day and the plan had always been to bring Raquel in as a 'plot twist'. The fans hadn't reacted particularly favorably, but Emory was smart. He'd been working to create a portrait of Raquel and while Alexander was spending time with a still recovering Porchia they went to work on creating a narrative for Porchia.

Alexander was supposed to spend a few days with Porchia and her family in Texas but that hadn't happened. And Porchia was content to have a weekend in San Diego.

Monday morning had arrived and Alexander was to meet Cashmere at the airport.

• • •

"These cameras are annoying," Raquel admitted. It hadn't been the first time. "I think every time anything even tried to cross my mind I remembered."

"Kind of like a birth control?"

Raquel used a pillow to hit Alexander, "Not at all." Raquel bit her lip and looked at Alexander. She gave a quick smile before she stood up. As she stretched Alexander watched the small sliver of skin. Hadn't there been a time he enjoyed the tease of it?

"Take a picture, it'll last longer," she said as she tossed a pillow at him which he caught. Raquel headed to the shower Alexander rewound the last several days. He hadn't a moment alone with Cashmere and she wasn't responding by text. But he wanted to talk to her, even if things between them were still unclear he wanted a chance to hear her thoughts.

"They are considering them both from what I heard," Raquel said as she took a sip of whiskey. "Doesn't matter who you choose, the offer is going to be put on the table. But at least you would have done your part."

Alexander had invited Raquel to the charity event; his auction item had been a session of legal advice from her with a website consultation from him. It was the best he could come up with having ignored Rick's suggestion of a private striptease. He suspected if he had Rick would have made sure to attend.

"What time's your flight?" Raquel yelled from the bathroom, starting the shower.

Alexander was flying straight to KC from San Diego and meeting Cashmere at the airport. At least he hoped he still was. Maybe she went completely rogue and off the grid.

"In a few hours."

A knock came at the door and Alexander knew who it was before he opened it.

"Ash. Frank." Makeup and camera. It was about that time. He sighed as he stepped to the side. "I haven't showered yet."

"You're welcome to join me," Raquel called out as she tossed her night tank top onto the bed from inside the bathroom. The suite was large, large enough that from the angle where they stood no one saw anything but it hadn't prevented a visual from transpiring.

"Excited to see her today?" Ash asked as he sat his bag down and began to rummage through it. Frank took up a space in the corner and said nothing as usual.

"Yeah, I'm ready,"

One moment Alexander saw Ash and by the next he was remembering another time—

Cashmere was absently smiling on the ride back. Everything had worked smoothly. Alexander negotiated on a solid plan for the bands website build and the launch of it as well as sold Ethan on a bill of goods that Grant would undoubtedly be pleased by. They were both in good moods as they headed toward the bar. Cashmere, too elated at all the possibility had forgotten all about her other interview, but they'd called to reschedule to see if she'd be open for coming tomorrow early in the morning. In too much of a good mood she'd accepted despite knowing her pension for early morning things tended to fall in the realm of the Easter Bunny and four-leaf clovers.

"So," Alexander said looking over at her, "Am I am still looking at my new assistant or just an unbelievably attractive young woman whose company I have the pleasure of keeping for a very short lived happy hour."

Cashmere looked over to Alexander, "Boldly flirting are we?"

He laughed, "I figure I only have so many more hours of your presence before the carriage turns back into a pumpkin and I'm just another lowly rat admiring a piece of cheese."

"That almost sounds like an indirect prude comment there Roth."

They arrived at a stoplight and he turned to face Cashmere, who had a mischievous grin gracing her face.

• • •

Everything felt right at the moment. Alexander wanted to reach over and caress her cheek. "How so?" he asked instead.

"Well you just compared me to a dairy product and that could be you indirectly wishing to stare at my derriere or because dairy, milk rather, comes from the breast of a cow you might be inferring you are a boob guy."

The light changed but Alexander couldn't move, he was too busy laughing; tears streamed down his face, "That is a stretch."

"Quite the leap you mean," Cashmere winked.

"Alexander," Ash snapped a finger in front of his face, "Still with us."

He nodded, his breath caught, as he exhaled a smile fell upon his face.

He was remembering.

Chapter 24

Cashmere

There was something surreal about being back home, sitting in the airport, and having a camera pointed directly at you. Instead of letting it bother her at this point, Cashmere chose to be still. Kate had gone off to the bathroom and there was about another hour before Alexander would arrive.

She still hadn't quite figured out how the next three days would go. She hadn't texted anyone. In many ways, she'd shut down. She replayed events in her mind but it wasn't until the airport and no one to truly distract her that she came to the realization why she'd felt off.

She reached for her phone to check her calendar and confirm that it wasn't PMS but she knew Aunt Flo wasn't to blame. She'd spent so much time chasing different things and being back in KC, put it all into perspective, the origins of the tale she hadn't realized she was living, repeating, consistently setting herself to attend to time and time again.

"It's been about two years," Cashmere started, she looked over to the camerawoman, who in turn said nothing. Cashmere observed the young woman and the dedication to which she focused on the task at hand. Dropping her head down and looking at her fingers, Cashmere continued, "do you know what it's like to slip so far into a void? I've always kept busy, you know, it was like buoys keeping me afloat. Do this with band. Get doe-eyed for this or that and I think back now, nothing was never enough. It couldn't be."

. . .

Cashmere blinked. She continued to blink and shook her head. She tucked her chin into her chest and whispered, "I don't want it..."

A page came across the intercom. Kate was still gone. Cashmere's hands had wound around the other, twisting and re-twisting until her skin became warm to the touch.

"I'm going to use the restroom. Can you keep an eye on my things?"

They replied nothing. As Cashmere got up, after a few feet, she noticed she hadn't been followed and was thankful for that. She headed out of the airport; she knew where she needed to go.

Back in the day she'd gone by Helen, her fighting name if you asked the right neighbor, but most called her Ms. Devers. As the uber driver pulled up to the two-family flat brick building Cashmere could see the neighborhood had aged. A couple of street lights weren't working and the lawn for one house was severely overgrown.

"Do you need me to stay?" the driver asked.

Cashmere laughed; the place did have a creepy feel to it. "I'm good. Thank you."

As she stepped out of the car, she made a mental note to give a tip. Once she climbed the rickety wooden stairs, she knocked on the familiar dark blue door. The sound felt like home.

Cashmere could see a cat at the window. Was that Juanita? Julia? Cashmere pored through her memory trying to remember all the cats and the various names. She knocked again but still no answer.

As she took a step, she submitted a tip for the driver and stared down the street. In the distance she saw a woman walking her dog. There was almost a double-step to her gait but the long skirt was a dead giver.

Cashmere walked down the steps to meet her, "Ms. Devers?"

The woman paused. Her dog stopped, a golden hair thing... Collie? Cashmere wondered. She wasn't a breed expert but the dog was friendly.

"Yeah. Who wants to know?" Ms. Devers narrowed her eyes and Cashmere had to fight back her laugh. It wasn't the time to joke. She saw how suspicious she was of her. And just as Ms. Devers reached into her pocket...

"It's me. Donna's daughter."

Ms. Devers face broke. A small smile slowly crossed her face revealing a missing tooth at the bottom and a gap Cashmere had forgotten about.

"Lil Cassie!? Oh Cassidy, now that's right. Chile! Now you know better being out here this late. Streetlights on and walking up on me like that. Female or not, you can catch it too."

Cashmere laughed at this as they walked back. "It's Cashmere now," she said as she took to the side with no railing and took the leash to help. Ms. Devers had to be in her late 70's or 80's by now and still she took her evening walk. But now with a companion.

"What's that now?" she huffed once they made it to the door. Cashmere noted her breath hadn't been fully caught yet and she waited until they were settled in the sitting room before she started again. Her phone buzzed but she ignored it.

"I changed my name. It's Cashmere now."

Ms. Devers looked up and the little wrinkles on her face folded into a frown. Her eyes stared upward as if she were thinking. But before she could catch hold of the thought a clatter from the mantle caused them both to stir.

"Damnit Marion, get down from there. And where's Georgia?"

As if the cat had heard its name, she brushed up against Ms. Devers' ankles.

"Oh no you don't, don't think I forgot about your gift from earlier. Y'all gone stop this foolishness. Be a dear and grab Audrey from the window. I'll find those other hussies later."

Cashmere did as she was instructed while Ms. Devers went to the kitchen. She took a seat in a chair with a tall back, it wasn't covered in plastic like the couch. She tried to recall had everything once been in plastic, but visits to Ms. Devers were often outside and, on the porch; she couldn't recall coming in frequently and if she had it wasn't farther than the entrance.

Ms. Devers returned to the room with two steaming cups. "Now what was that about cash?"

"Oh, I was saying my name is Cashmere now. I changed it."

"Again?" Ms. Devers said as she handed the cup to Cashmere and took a seat on the plastic sofa. "Donna an' nem changed it too. She told it to me once. Can't remember now. You know that Daddy of yours not on the block no' mo. Him and the new wife moved awhile back. Felt like I was just telling that to someone not too long ago. They stopped taking in kids. Think it broke your Daddy's heart, but that had always been his and Donna's thing."

Cashmere nodded. Her foster mom had lost her battle with cancer. Things had been a struggle before but it was even more complicated once she passed. Cashmere rarely called or made visits. And this was the truth of her loneliness, the idea she'd always be someone's rejection.

"I heard Donna once say, that that mama of yours, y'kno the one that actually birthed ya before she handed you off to a sister had made contact. Lied and said she tracked down your real daddy and they wanted a visit."

Cashmere had learned, and never forgotten, that it was good to just listen when it came to Ms. Devers. But these were things she'd never heard before and there wasn't much she remembered from her early childhood, before being taken in by the Smith's.

"Listen to me. What brings you by? I thought I heard you'd moved out East. Got into a school out there? Wilma, come here kitty."

Cashmere watched as Wilma, a tabby, strolled right out of the room instead.

"Crazy bit-"

"Yes! But only for about a year. Then I moved to California and finished-"

"Oh! I remember now. They were so close together now. That makes three y'know. With you coming to visit ole Helen. Can't remember dem otha folk but that boy, Sanjay? Rodriquez? Shit, they were the only family on the block. Stayed with you for a bit while his parents got a fixin' to uh... now what was it"

Cashmere's phone had buzzed back to back to back for the last five minutes. As she took it from her pocket she heard Ms. Devers gasp.

"SARAH! Get down from there this instance."

As Cashmere looked at the missed calls she noticed the messages from Alexander and her heart skipped a beat.

I've arrived.

I remembered something.

At hotel. Can we talk?

Cashmere knew she should respond. She'd been ignoring him for the better part of a week now. As she stood up, she knew she couldn't put it off any longer.

"Thank you for the tea Ms. Devers."

"Oh, so soon? Well it is late. What brought you by?"

Cashmere saw the worrisome look. She wondered if Ms. Devers was worried she'd been a bad host or if the woman thought she might be asking for help. Or something else.

"I was in town for the next few days. And just wanted to see a friendly face."

Ms. Devers raised her brow and quipped her lips, "Well I don't know about that. A lie if there ever was one. Ain't nuthin friendly about this face but I'll let you be chile. I'm just glad to see you. Like I said felt right considering them other recent visits. And I'll tell them what I told you. Last I heard your mama was in St. Louis. Your Daddy probably knows more."

Cashmere, having returned to the moment, fully aware took in the words. "Who came by?"

"I told you, um Sanchez and some other folk."

Cashmere hadn't recognized either name. Her phone buzzed again. She silenced it and put out a request for an uber.

"Do you remember anything about these other folk?"

Ms. Devers looked toward the hall light. Another cat descended the staircase just as Marion and Georgia hopped onto the couch beside her. She rubbed them both as they settled in her lap.

"All fine looking folk really. Didn't seem bad. Like I said the one was with y'all for the one summer. Family had some issues with the government and he stayed while they went away for a bit. You know Wes and Donna were good."

A name struck Cashmere's head then, but it wasn't possible so she let it go just as quickly.

"Them others, well they had a recorder, and them crazy box phones. Asked if I was okay to be on camera for an interview."

Cashmere hadn't seen Emory as often but even he wouldn't stoop this low. He'd ask first he wouldn't just go digging... But a tiny voice instead Cashmere's head whispered *the other Emory would.*

"Do you remember anything else? Did any of them leave a card or way to reach out?"

"Oh yeah, the camera folk did. But Marion was being pissy then."

Cashmere didn't press further, she'd just have to go to the source. First, she'd tackled Alexander then Emory. Things were shifting or had shifted and it was harder for her to ignore that change was coming. Something inside her was sparking.

Her phone chimed to let her know her ride was approaching.

"Cassidy, girl, you're looking good. I'd always been worried about you amongst the other ones. Always to yourself but look at you girl. Just look at you. You're doing good. But you don't need me to tell you that." Ms. Devers smiled as she opened the door. "Take care child."

Cashmere reached forward to give her a hug. Her original intentions on coming might have been to fill a void but she'd left with something more somehow. Seeing Ms. Devers with her cats, she wasn't an old lady alone.

Ms. Devers had made a choice. Found her own bit of peace. Cashmere wasn't alone. She could find hers too.

● ● ●

Chapter 25

Alexander

It felt like a showdown. That an ultimatum needed to be issued and that it was coming from both fronts. He sat hunched over the bar and waited. He had a seat facing the hotel bar's entrance that gave him prime viewing advantage. He'd sent Cashmere another text, letting her know she could find him there if she wanted to talk.

That had been an hour ago. It was late and he feigned going to bed early to ensure privacy. Though it hadn't seemed to matter. Cashmere was likely a no show.

A woman saddled up to Alexander. It hadn't been the first time since he arrived.

"What's your story cowboy?"

For a moment he pictured it was Cashmere asking the question. A smile so strong that it'd reflect from her eyes the same amount of warmth that filled him. For someone who couldn't remember much he was drawn to her, desperate for that reaction, and most of all he just wanted to be alone with her without the cameras.

"I'm waiting for someone."

"I know. You told me that earlier."

Alexander turned to look at the woman and he hadn't recognized her but the hair seemed familiar.

Alexander got up from the stool and threw back the last bit of alcohol, requested another and tossed it back just as quickly.

● ● ●

"Woo, okay, you want my advice?"

Alexander hadn't answered. He was sure he just wanted to sleep at this point and figured the alcohol would help do the trick. He'd booked a separate hotel room intending to give Cashmere space, unbeknownst to the crew that was with them. He at least wanted to talk to her about that but it seemed even it could not be managed.

The woman turned on her stool and rubbed Alexander's arm, he'd opted to buy a Royal's t-shirt while at the airport as a souvenir and potential conversation starter with Cashmere, back when he thought they'd at least have dinner tonight.

"Forget about her," the woman said.

Alexander took one final shot and settled his bill. "That's the problem."

He gave a smile as he walked away. Once in the lobby he thought he saw her. That the air carried her scent. He floated toward the elevators but they were too slow. He walked to the door that led to the steps and began the climb. He heard her laugh as it echoed down below. Taunting him.

When he reached his floor and made his way to his door he fetched around for a key card, mumbling a half-remembered song. He reached for the light but it was already on. As he made his way across the suite something tripped up his mind as well as his feet. He stumbled, the wall catching his fall.

He collapsed on the bed, his eyes opened as sounds hit him. Questions that really should be answered came and went. He'd left the light on? The tv? A black lace bra on the bed?

Questions, important as they were, none seemed to click long enough until from out the bathroom came one Cashmere, wet, with only a pale-yellow towel wrapped around her body. Alexander, previously flopped on his stomach, shot up and their eyes were on the other.

Words came. Words went. She was here. His eyes roamed, her hair was dripping wet and he wanted to touch it, touch her. He wasn't sure how it happened but one moment he'd been by the bed and by the next he was on his feet, close to her. "Cass."'

She turned around. Her eyes no longer on his before she sighed and looked back at him. "Yes."

He shook his head in disbelief. This wasn't really happening. It was just another fantasy and he laughed for thinking otherwise. He stepped back. Signaling with his hands from his eyes to hers and smiled. This wasn't real but still.

"I think I'm in love with you Cashmere Watson." He said falling back onto the bed. Sleep found him easily. He hoped more memories would find him. He hoped he would be able to speak with her tomorrow. But he wished mostly to hold her.

Alexander and Cashmere strolled into the nightclub, Tainted. The two side by side, so close, that anyone who saw them would not be mistaken in believing they were a couple. Alexander welcomed the assumption.

"Apartment flooded?" Cashmere offered.

"Wasn't that used on 'The Office'?"

"I could arrange for someone to call me about my very sick Lucifer."

"Who's Lucifer?" Alexander asked, reaching for her hand.

"My imaginary pet."

"Or we could just show our faces and gradually break off, meet out here in say fifteen minutes?"

Alexander watched as the cogs in Cashmere's head turned, they were both working to ensure the most fail-safe appropriate excuse to bail on the happy hour.

"Casalex," she murmured.

"What?"

Squeezing his hand, "nothing."

"Casalex."

Alexander was waking, the word on his mind but only temporarily. Warmth. As his body awakened he noted an imbalance. A chill from his exposed flesh, when had he gotten undressed? But warmth from the body wrapped in his arms... Had he?

There'd been people at the bar but he was sure he hadn't come back with anyone. Had he sleepwalked for company to occupy him for the night?

It was late. Or very early, Alexander thought depending on who you were. As his eyes adjusted to the dark an awareness took shape and the more he took in the present, the more tiny details found meaning. The moment her name came to mind it was as if all the supporting evidence flooded to his mind for confirmation.

Her scent. The wavy hair that tickled his left forearm. She was using it as part of her pillow. The shape of her that Alexander could now trace. His free hand lightly moving to her hip, the inclination to squeeze and bring her even closer to him. His head nuzzled near her neck, taking in a deep breath, just in case. Already fear had found him.

This could be the last time.

Memories he'd thought were dreams—Cashmere in nothing but a towel wet, her in a shirt and boxers pulling his clothes off, the suggestions he'd made about her undressing him, the sympathetic eyes, the kiss on the cheek, and her convinced to rest beside him. Her whispering to him. "We've got a condition here. It's called-"

"Casalex," he repeated into her ear. He'd remembered a bit more. Was it a coincidence that she'd said it to him during his recovering drunken state?

Cashmere still slept. There were a million ways his body responded to the nearness of her. The scent of her alone. He carefully reached for the sheet at his side and lightly covered them both. He moved in closer. Not letting her go, something in him had decided.

There was a draw. There always had been and even if he never remembered, he wasn't going to ignore it. Some things were worth pursuing.

When Alexander woke again, his arms empty, Cashmere gone but the crew was at the door; he was ready. The pursuit had already begun.

Chapter 26

Cashmere

She hesitated outside the door. There was a lot to make up for. Apologies owed. The coffee crate rattled. She took a deep breath, quelling her fears and hoping to get control of her shaky hands. The box of donuts in her other hand, she knocked on the door.

This hadn't been the first time she felt the nerves of her anxiety threaten to make her breakout. She'd visited Kate's room earlier with breakfast and an apology. Kate wasn't pleased but then again it was five in the morning.

She was off to an early start and she needed it if these next days were to go off as they needed to. Or as close to it as she could get, there'd always be a level of unpredictability as she tackled things. With her pinky finger she pressed the doorbell.

As the seconds ticked away she thought she'd seen movement from a bush but upon closer inspection there was nothing. Another few moments passed and no one answered. She tried the doorbell again and still after a spell nothing happened. There was no movement to indicate anyone was there.

She sat the coffee down on the big country porch. How was it they hadn't any chairs and table out here? It begged for seating.

Cashmere knocked on the door. As she took in her surroundings, this house was a lot different from the one she'd been raised in. For one it was in the middle of nowhere, far away from the city. It was a great place, if you had a big family to let the kids roam and animals run the gamut but the new wife had kids that were grown, no interest in fostering or animals.

These things hadn't bothered Cashmere. They stood out and told a story but nothing she put to fault. Instead it made her feel a certain way about her place. Something she'd wrestled with all her life and only magnified when her father, foster dad, remarried. She'd never been good with keeping up with the others as well. It was as if the island of Cashmere, in time, had only grown more narrow, selective.

Was it wrong? She wondered as time ticked by and no one answered. It never occurred to her, until that very moment, they might not be in town. But she'd known that if she'd bothered to check, to keep in touch.

She thought to leave the items on the porch but realized that might not be the brightest idea. It was still too early and even her own mind wasn't awake enough. As she took a seat on the top step, she opened the uber app. The service wasn't great, as the app loaded, she looked up and for the second time she'd thought she'd seen movement near one of the hedges.

Not curious enough to check it out, she was set to confirm her uber when a padlock sounded and she turned around. Standing in the doorway in a shiny pink satin robe was a woman.

Cashmere stood up, brushing off her jeans and having trouble with words. How was she to address her?

"Hi," she said, extending her now sweaty hands.

"Good morning," the woman side. She pulled on her robe a bit more and her eyes closed in on Cashmere. "You look familiar, were you hear last week about the couch?"

The woman, Lynn, owned her silver hair. Her brown skin and warm smile, she was fit for the cover of Ebony, the sexy in silver edition.

"Yes. Aw, yes I am."

Lynn looked down, having noticed the coffee and donuts. Cashmere observed she politely avoided asking about it.

"Uh, ah, this is for you."

"Oh," Lynn said. Cashmere picked up the food and handed it to her. "What do we owe-"

"Nothing. No reason. My church often encourages us to be part of the community and do friendly gestures. And I was so impressed with you and your husband last week that I wanted to show my appreciation."

Lynn, who'd had her hands out to take the items slowly retracted them, a frown marring her face. "My husband?"

"Mom, who's at the door?" A female voice from the back answered.

"My husband," Lynn smiled. "Yes, I'll have to wake Wesley. He loves donuts. How'd you know?"

"Mom," came the insistent voice again.

It was at this moment a strange lurking, a quiet chasm, quaked through Cashmere.

Another woman, in her 40's or early 50's perhaps, came to the door. Her dark hair pulled into a ponytail. "May I help you?"

Lynn, as she held the donuts now, lifted them toward the woman, "Look Lexie, she brought Wes's favorite. She's a church girl. Her church delivered it to us. Isn't that nice?"

Lexie's eyes narrowed for a moment before recognition took place. "You're the baby girl, the last one?"

"I'll go wake Wesley," Lynn said.

Lexie rubbed smooth touches across her mother's shoulder, "Mama, how about you go take these back to the kitchen okay?"

"That's a good idea, baby, then I'll go get Wesley."

Lexie smiled and patted her mother before she returned her gaze back to Cashmere.

Cashmere, for her part, held her ground. She was still standing. She wanted to run. Like she always had. She was sure that's what she needed to do. She didn't need to stick around for this part.

"Cassidy, right?" Lexie asked, there was a sad smile there.

Cashmere didn't want the pity. She didn't want the hurt. She didn't want to know. She didn't want this confirmation... She hadn't planned on-

"I'm so sorry honey. No one had a good number for you and hadn't a way to reach you..."

All this time...

All these years.

Cashmere had fought to carve something of her own. She'd thought that's what she'd been doing. Focused to become something. Removing herself from everyone, the world she never felt had been hers or the family and now-

"...he'd been sick..."

The world was still moving-

"...it was a tough call but the others felt..."

It always did. It would. And yet-

"... mama hasn't been right since, it's hard for her..."

Cashmere's just had stopped.

Chapter 27

Alexander

To anyone else it seemed business as usual. The crew had done some scenic shots, catching the sunrise and taking Alexander around KC while Kate and a recently arrived Jazmine called Cashmere.

At around 11am they were back at the hotel. Twenty minutes later so was Cashmere.

Jazmine sighed with relief. Kate gave her a dirty look. Cashmere came bearing more apologetic treats, at least it felt as such for Kate, who'd informed everyone of her morning wakeup. Alexander watched as she Cashmere skillfully dodged questions. Her demeanor was so different yet nothing short of belief. She was capable of being nice so no questioned her as she praised everyone.

She worked her way toward Alexander, she'd caught his eye a couple times. For his part he'd returned each look, meaning behind each glance but he could not deter away from the feeling that something felt off.

"And for you Mr. Roth, my deepest apology yet since I stood you up last night and appeared to get a bit of amnesia myself when it came to returning text, a cheese-danish and blueberry scone."

Her smile was big. The camera's were going. She was throwing out ideas for the day, changes to the plan to spice things up. And no one said a thing. No one thought it strange. It occurred to Alexander maybe they thought she was trying to overcompensate for all the other times she'd been a terrible participant. Or perhaps this was what she'd intended all along. It was a faux imposed love for the sake of a show. Now that she was in the final three, she wanted to pull a few tricks from out of her sleeve. Whatever the case, no one questioned it, they all went along. But somehow, he knew this was Cashmere's best performance to date.

Pretending everything was okay.

The evening was cool. Cashmere was even cooler. They'd spent some time shopping downtown. Cashmere telling stories of her childhood but when asked about visiting her family, she only smiled and wrapped an arm in his.

"Excited about the game today?"

It was strange. As they sat down and watched the baseball game, this was the type of thing Alexander had thought should be happy. His eyes peeked at her from the corner, she took a bite of her hot dogs and as she caught him, offered him a bite.

"QA inspected, no poison found, sir," she said waving the dog in front of him. He raised a brow and she matched the skeptical look. He took her hand in his and angled the hot dog, taking a huge bite.

"Hey!" Her outrage was cute. As Alexander chewed, she took back her hot dog, or what remained of it. "Consider that your one and only bite."

He knew, somehow, this wasn't real. That there was something just below the surface and he was conflicted. Not knowing how to address it nor wanting to ruin this moment. There was the chance he was wrong.

As the game progressed Alexander let go more, getting more comfortable. First he reached to hold her hand, she leaned on his shoulder and even though she wore jeans, shirt and a light jacket, he offered up his.

"Where were you earlier, really?"

She stiffened. Her hand clammy. But she was saved. "Oh, look!"

She pointed to the screen, the Kiss Cam, which had zeroed in on them. She looked at Alexander and he shook his head.

"Oh, come on, you know you wanna..."

She leaned in and kissed him on the lips. It was soft. A light feathery touch. Cashmere was right. He did want to. And a taste wasn't enough.

From the surrounding cheers, everyone else wanted to see them too.

"I want to pick you." Alexander wasn't sure where it'd come from or why he said. But it was out there. Cashmere was quick. The shock disappeared as soon as she remembered to smile.

"Once upon a time," she whispered, "so did I."

"At least we brought home a winner," Cashmere said as they exited the cab and made their way through the hotel. They hadn't walked hurriedly. The two camera team followed along with Jazmine who was texting with Emory laying out the last few days.

Taking Cashmere's hand at the elevator Alexander said, "It's almost over. Sad or happy to have your life back?"

"What life?"

Something about those words hit in a way, in an authentic sense than anything else today.

"What's going on?" He leaned in, hoping it wouldn't be picked up by the audio, but she only shook her head.

Alexander looked behind them and chose not to press any further as they boarded the elevator. They rode up in silence. He walked her to the door, the cameras still following and once in the room they bid everyone goodnight. He'd begun to release his hand from Cashmere's but she held on tighter. They stood there at the door, neither moving.

"I can give a few minutes, then head back."

She shook her head; her eyes were moist with unshed tears. He hadn't understood, something was wrong.

"Stay," she whispered moving closer to him, her free hand came to rest on his chest and she looked up at him. Her eyes looking into his before moving to his lips. She pressed further and Alexander, like a magnet, moved in even harder.

Releasing her hand he gripped her waist. She sighed and Alexander knew. If he had any will power, now was the time to use it. He backed away slowly.

"I want to," she said, moving toward him.

His body responded as if it had been the only thing it had ever wanted to hear. The only thing it needed to. Both hands were on her, his lips on hers, and his body raged. Anxious to feel her, to be inside her, to be consuming all that was and would ever be.

He wanted it all. Based on Cashmere's moans, so did she. The two would have continued if not for a series of events: The knock that came at the door and the phone rang.

But this was all noise. What had really happened had been the dam that finally cracked...

Alexander looked at Cashmere, the tears she could no longer fight off. Something stirred in his heart, his hands clenched the sheets, his breath momentarily staggered then caught. This moment right now was painful. It resonated with him. Perhaps there was a part of him that would always recognize what it was to hurt.

To be broken.

Chapter 28

Cashmere

I want to pick you...

The words rang in Cashmere's mind. Not the almost sexual encounter. She avoided thinking about her foster parents. Not even the kiss that still lingered on her lips as her and Alexander parted.

KC had not gone how she thought it would. She hadn't had much of a plan but she thought, part of her wanted to show Alexander her childhood home. She'd pictured what it would be like walking the old neighborhood but she hadn't factored how much the ghost of past decisions would haunt her so.

I want to pick you...

You.

"You're quiet."

"Just tired."

Cashmere and Art hadn't spoken much. Text yes. But she'd kept her distance. His sudden offer to pick her up from the airport seemed to come out of the blue, she hadn't pressed because part of her was curious about the band. The night of auction and her time spent with Dallas hadn't brought her any closer to knowing what was going on.

"How's the new band assistant?"

"An interesting guy," Art said. Forever gallant.

"Dallas called him a turd."

"When did you…" Art stopped. Cashmere regretted mentioning him just as soon as the words had left her mouth. "He's okay. He's not you for sure."

"So what have you been up to?"

"You mean besides pining over my unrequited love for… tacos?"

She smiled and adjusted her seatbelt. She'd made the mistake of grabbing an old bra when packing and currently had a uni-boob going on which the seatbelt could not circumnavigate.

"Writing a lot of songs mostly. Thinking about how to make this better."

"What better?"

"Us."

Cashmere reached for the radio dial and Art did at the same time. Except his hand caught hers.

"Cashmere…"

"You don't have to say anything."

"Not even an apology?"

"Not even that."

Art pulled over his jeep. His hand still clutched hers. "Look, I'm not sure what's going on in your head. Honestly I'm afraid to truly know the wiring of a woman's head, particularly yours but I do know that given everything going on, once you've had some time, after this over, maybe we can talk more?"

Cashmere looked at Art. His eyes earnest. The way he looked at her now. He squeezed her hand.

"Okay," she said. "Okay," she repeated. He smiled and kissed her hand. He held onto it, all the way back to her place. They rode in silence the rest of the way.

Cashmere wasn't sure how the time had moved so fast yet so slow. One moment she was dropped off at home and on the couch, before she knew it was time to record Alexander's decision.

Emory had stopped by the house. His eyes roamed the place she occupied on the couch, the light from her phone, all was dark. He tilted his head and she returned her eyes back to her screen watching the episode of Alexander with Porchia. She caught a clip, a preview of his time with Raquel, and decided her level of self-torture had limits.

"I'm going to lay out an outfit for you," he'd said. She winced. "I have something... we need to talk."

Here it was, she thought, he was going to admit about sneaking around to get additional intel. That he'd secretly spied on her, tapped her phone, had been in KC, and was preparing to reveal the sob story of a foster kid still utterly lost.

He flicked on a light and she hissed.

"What are you? A cat now? Girl get up. I don't know what's going on and why you are moping but I'd think you'd be happy for it to be almost over."

She hadn't sat up. Her eyes followed Emory as he came to sit on the white loveseat.

"First, I want you to know that I turned down Trevor's offer."

She blinked, blinked again, and noticed she'd reached the part of the episode where Porchia and Alexander sat on a park bench, him enjoying ice cream, her eyes watched his every lick and just as she leaned in for a kiss a group of kids with water guns ran by stopping the moment and destroying the vibe.

Cashmere wanted to laugh at this part every time she watched. Something in her said to laugh, even if it wasn't Porchia, it was still hilarious.

"I was there, you know," Emory said interrupting her thought. "Me and Jazmine worked together on the timeline for when Alexander was with Raquel and which of us would be there. I took on being the producer on the ground for Porchia's. By choice."

She looked at the screen on final time before she set her phone down. She closed her eyes and pulled the blanket around her tighter.

"They came to me. About a spinoff. The ratings are really good and they want to do a more involved take on the network and asked me specifically. I know Trevor spoke to you but he probably didn't get deep into details."

She remembered that visit. Trevor had come by. He was a 'big fan' of hers and was asking about what she'd planned next. A lot of the girls had gigs lined up, some more than others. But this had never interested Cashmere. Even the fan pages and profiles for her were managed by staff, she wasn't interested in that kind of engagement.

"Are you with me still?"

She closed her eyes in response.

"I turned it down because while I think the concept is fun and could be good for you. I think you need something else. Plus, seeing as you never remembered one tiny detail I'd rather not have our friendship suffer any longer for plans made while the other is intoxicated."

Emory got up from the couch and started to walk off. "I just thought you should know."

"When?"

Her voice was low, scratchy. She cleared her throat and again said, "when?"

"When what?"

"When did you decline Trevor's offer?"

Emory narrowed his eyes, "It doesn't matter. I did."

It had mattered. He knew it. And so, did Cashmere. Emory started to walk off again as Cashmere sat up.

"I do remember."

Emory's back to her, he stopped.

"I remembered a while ago. But you won't get an apology from me. You know better than to ask me things when I'm intoxicated."

Emory turned around a smirk on his face, "consider us even." He walked off to his bedroom then.

To Cashmere it was still off balance but it hadn't mattered. Outside of her own; she had one more heart to break.

Chapter 29

Alexander

I want to pick you...

Alexander had said those words. He'd bared a truth and it still hadn't felt right. Once back in his room he retrieved his journal and sifted through the entries. Some more intact than others.

He wanted to reach out to Cashmere but she needed space. Plus tonight was the night. A knock came at the door and without having to be told, the fact alone of knowing where his mind had been just a second ago—he knew. Plans had changed.

"Alexander?"

"It's open Jazmine."

"They are cutting back. We are combining the reunion and the pick all tomorrow."

A wave coursed through Alexander, like a release. Maybe it was because he suspected there'd be a schedule change or the fact those words, that particular entry had been the one he'd seen before closing the journal.

"Why?"

He wanted to see her today. He didn't want another day for something to happen. To change what he wanted to do. A lot could happen in the time it took from now until the show.

"Emory suggested it. They are still working on the footage from you and Cashmere's time together and hope to air it tonight. It's all hands on deck."

"But…" Alexander felt his face scrunch. There'd always been about a 2-3 day gap from when something was taped to when it aired on the web. Why the sudden rush?

"Can you be down in five? We're going to do some shoots with you and Rick. Put on your outfit for that last show still. Just be careful… well no, maybe not." Jazmine paused as she looked to the ceiling looking for an answer.

"Just put on something nice. Save the last show wear for tomorrow. Some of the girls have arrived tonight to stay over rather than arrive tomorrow. We're going to do a dinner and social later if you want to join."

"Who's all here?"

Jazmine's eyes were sad. "She's not here. Alexander, you should know-"

A knock at the door stopped Jazmine. Emory entered, out of breath and he looked between the two. Alexander noticed Jazmine stiffen but she said nothing else.

"Hey, you two, we've run into a snag with some footage. Jazmine, I need your input since you were there. Alexander you're welcome too. Did you tell him?"

Jazmine fingers twitched at her sides. "Yeah, we're good to go to do everything tomorrow. I was just telling Alexander that some girls arrived back today and we were planning to do a social tonight."

"Oh okay, cool cool. I just left from seeing Cashmere. I picked an outfit out for her and told her about the change but I'm not sure she'll come. She's been in a strange headspace. What all happened in KC?"

Jazmine poked Emory in the chest, "Guess you'll find out when the footage airs tonight." She stuck out her tongue and started to leave but turned around to Alexander, "See you later?"

Alexander gave a thumbs up. Nodding, Jazmine left the room. Emory hung back and stepped further into the bedroom.

"Well it's about that time, approaching the end zone. Got any last words?" Emory pretended to hold up an old fashion filming camera, his hand rolling it from the side.

"Be careful what you wish for…"

The evening arrived.

Cashmere was a great actress; she'd really missed her calling. But she wore her sadness even better. So well, in fact, that Alexander questioned rather it might be real or not. All the other girls had had their moment but of course she'd been saved for last.

Rick started to open his mouth, his hand directing Cashmere to take her seat but her mouth was open, "You're still in love with her Ernie," she started and there were a few audible gasp but no shock was greater than that of Alexander's. He hid his expression, his face a solid mask of nothing as he tried to work the angle. There was a purpose here, nothing short of dramatics without some underlying reason, was it a last minute scripted change?

"It had never been right to bring me back, not if there's nothing to begin with because you and I both know you're not ready," her voice broke on the last word.

Everything was a lie. Except that. "I won't be a pity pick and be 'chosen' just so they can get their show, so they can get their fat girl ratings spike. I'm no one's pawn. Not even yours."

This was what it was like Alexander imagined. To be in the seat of a car and not behind the driver's wheel. To be both the passenger and the deer caught in the headlight just before it crashed.

"It's always been her," Cashmere continued. It was something then, maybe the flick of her eyes or movement to the side but Alexander saw that Raquel was standing on the balcony. He hadn't even felt the moment she entered. He was sure there was something in Cashmere that gave it away. He noted that once he made contact with Raquel she immediately nodded, the cameras hadn't caught it, at least he hoped they hadn't. "Even now, it's her and I'm not up for playing second string."

Alexander's eyes narrowed. For the first time ever he couldn't distinguish what was real and what was fake. It was at the moment, poor timing as the crew in charge of video playback did a montage of scenes of Alexander's and Cashmere's time together. It went by in a flash until a moment he'd never known shown. Cashmere eyes were focused on him instead even though there was video feed directly in front of her, Rick watched.

"Cashmere, darling, come have a seat," Rick said, "Don't embarrass the poor fellow by messing that pretty face up."

"I'm leaving," Cashmere said. Alexander watched two Cashmere's- the bee before him and the bee that snuck into Porchia's room. An episode he'd watched of a memory he still hadn't recalled.

"... You can come if you're ready but spare me your confusion if you're not there."

"Spare you," Alexander said, his voice breaking. He watched as Raquel decided to make her way toward them, Rick was a bundle of nerves barely able to contain his glee. Alexander cleared his throat, "I could say the same to you Cass. Are you ready? Surely?"

Alexander flicked an eye to the door just waiting for the moment Art would come out as if it were a bad Jerry Springer episode and everyone's secret lover bombarded the stage. He hadn't said Art's name, nor Dallas, nor any other person he was sure Cashmere's had likely ever considered.

Cashmere stood still. Alexander heard from his earpiece the spike of ratings, the meme's shared, what was trending, the hashtags, and the possibility of the spinoff. No, even if there was doubt at the very moment between him and Cashmere. Her breathing was ragged. She was fighting back something; she was hurting and he wasn't sure if he could stop it. The wound was there, fresh as ever and they were both bleeding out but still trying to protect the other and themselves in the process.

Before Alexander could elaborate on the spoken, "It's not you," he'd said aloud at the same time that Cashmere suddenly proclaimed, "I know who the mole is."

Everyone paused as Cashmere drew a breath, blinked back tears as she stood facing Alexander before she shook her head and turned away. She took the seat Rick had continually offered her finally and to him asked, "I just want to be sure that the agreement is still as it stands with whoever correctly guesses the mole."

Rick looked away trying to catch the attention of a Producer even as Alexander heard the same confirmation in his ear piece. Though it didn't appear Rick was excited about the answer, "Yes" he hissed.

Alexander suddenly wondered what the penalty might be for guessing it wrong, he was sure there was something in the contract that might tie Cashmere down further than she wanted to be. Stepping toward the stage into the bright light he took a seat beside Cashmere, "You don't have to do this."

She looked at Alexander and smiled. A show Exec stepped onto the stage then holding an envelope, Alexander still was unsure about the events, this part seemed staged, too calculated to just be happening.

Rick stood to shake hands with the woman, smiling at the camera, "To our fabulous viewers this is our most esteemed Executive Producer Lauren Fields and in this envelope is the name of the mole. If our lovely Cashmere guesses correctly then our live show could very well be the last show," Rick hmphed with a fake smile riding his lips.

Raquel was just off set. Despite being part of the show, the final three, she was staged to the side to walk on after all the original 18 contestants had had their turn in the spotlight. Alexander watched as he she held her position but she was ready, at the slight inclination he knew she'd join him.

"It's Ash, the makeup artist," Cashmere announced without hesitation. And she hadn't waited either. Alexander watched as she stood up, walked away and retreated to the deck where he noticed there were arms that quickly enveloped her. They were Emory's. Alexander wondered just then, he wanted to make for her but Raquel came to sit beside him and she kissed his cheek.

The rest of the night came at a blur as the mole was confirmed, as Raquel held his hand, as Rick muffled about his contract and other things just slowly faded to the back. Things deconstructed. Things fell apart. Things hadn't gone as planned. Nothing was as it seemed and in all of it the one thing that felt clear about the events was Cashmere had been right. Alexander steamrolled toward decisions out of obligation. He wasn't ready to come to terms with that person he'd been. Maybe that was why he still hadn't remembered much. He wasn't the same person that was ready to let go. The person that wanted something different from the world and of his life. The person he thought he'd been ready to become.

He wasn't ready.

But now he also saw that she hadn't been ready either.

Chapter 30

Two Hours Earlier

Cashmere was fully prepared to lock herself in her room for the remainder of the evening but it appeared that Emory had plans of his own including jimmying the lock of her door and letting himself in after ten minutes had passed. He'd been at the door, yelled his threats, and made the walls of their house quiver.

"CASHMERE MEREDITH WATSON if you don't answer this door now," he yelled, for what would be his last time before going quiet for the length of time it took for him to retrieve his weapons of mass break in.

"Asshole," Emory said pushing the door open. Cashmere hadn't been sure if the word had been intended for her or the door. Still in her pink camisole and cotton pajama bottom, she took the nearest pillow to her head.

"You're impossible," Emory said as he reached over and yanked the pillow over, "Look, this is serious."

"Is it about that stupid show you blackmailed me into being on?"

"You mean that stupid show you originally agreed to be on while drunk, then later tried to back out of, only to remember YOU AGREED TO BE ON IT, and still decided to be an ass about it?"

"No," Cashmere stated simply. "No, I won't be part of your evil plans of reality show domination or whatever brand of lies Rick has sold you on. He's the mole isn't he? I bet he's the mole isn't he."

Emory shook his head and threw his hands across his face, with his eyes covered he growled his frustration, "Would you just stop thinking I'm out to get you? I'm not here to blackmail you."

"Emory, seriously, not tonight. I'll be gone and out of your life- forever, before you know it."

The sigh that escaped Emory's lips was strong enough to rattle the chain suspended from the ceiling fan. "He's going to choose you."

I want to pick you...

Cashmere hadn't said anything. She sat up looking at Emory, her eyes narrowed and her butt firmly rooted to the bed. She wouldn't be moving from this space.

"But you knew this already. And so does everyone else. So let me tell you another story instead of a time a friend went out on a limb for another and in doing so set him on a path of deceit just to become free. The friend that went out on a limb, let's call him E, E did this knowing his friend-"

"Stop with the bull Emory and get to the point."

Emory huffed, "The point is, Cass, you believed I was blackmailing until you realized you were just much part of this. That favor that I blackmail you with came at a price and that person is cashing in. It wasn't easy to *fix* that situation from a couple years back. In fact, had you just listened to me none of us would really be in this position."

Cashmere knew she should ask but her head hurt. She wasn't ready for more riddles and complications. "What is it Emory? Really what do you want?"

"Do you want him?"

"Why does it matter to you?"

"It doesn't really, but I know it matters to you so I care. And he's about to make a big decision on your behalf."

Cashmere sighed and leaned in further, "I'm listening."

"I need you to come."

"I got that."

"They're banking on you coming."

"Okay," Cashmere said, scooting to the edge of her bed and getting up to head over to her walk-in closet.

"Once he picks you," Emory started.

"The original planned first twist would've been for the final three ex's boyfriends being invited if I remember the contract right."

"Exactly."

"And then the second twist would've been Raquel becoming an option."

"That's right but then that got changed around due to the accident," Emory inched forward, "But do you know the last one?"

"Well, no, I always assumed the third twist would come with the reveal of the mole."

"No, from the beginning there had always been a clause in all contestants' contracts for an extension if chosen."

Cashmere's face twisted, "Meaning..."

"Don't be coy, you know what it means. Another three weeks of torture, Alexander as a contestant, except it'll be you sitting across Rick."

Cashmere considered his words. "Does Alexander know about this?"

Emory shrugged, "Maybe. I'm not sure if Raquel planned on letting him know. She knew only so much too, mostly from a legal standpoint but she's roped in because there are a few people betting her favor."

"Didn't realize this became a gambling pool."

"It's part of one of the online attachments Ash set up."

"I thought he only did makeup."

"Cashmere," Emory said. "You're stalling."

"No," she said, "I'm not. You've basically just told me I'm screwed. If I don't show they'll go on anyway. Alexander can..." she stopped.

Here it was. An answer, her loop, the thing which repeated in her life. Always reactive. Here now, was an opportunity to be strategic in how she played the game of life.

"The extension," Cashmere started, "So it actually doesn't end once he chooses, and my guess is they'll drag him all the way to the end."

"You're all signed on until December..."

She rolled her eyes as she flung a yellow dress onto the bed, "Nothing is ever simple. So what do you want me to do?"

Emory smiled, "Do what you do best Rogue One."

Cashmere shook her head and watched as Emory stepped out of her room, "I love this Emory the most," she said catching his eyes.

"Me too," he said before closing her door.

Cashmere discarded her lounge wear and sauntered over to her vanity. She applied her mascara and into the mirror she practiced the face she planned on exhibiting. The frown may be false, she thought, but the tears will be real. There was so much she'd been avoiding. So much she hadn't wanted to tackle and if she were honest she was thankful for the distraction of the show. Alexander. His decision. But now it was time for her to choose a new path.

It was time to let go...

Epilogue

Baseball season was coming to a close. Fall was around the corner. The wind rustled the treetops with the promise of cooler temperatures. Alexander slipped his shades from his buzzed cut top and back onto his eyes as he stood in line for a hot dog. He craved a stadium hot dog. There was something about them that tasted better than any grilled attempts he made at home. But food truck hot dogs were just as good.

He still needed to make his way to the nacho food truck to order grilled chicken and veggies. Raquel was on some carb, low fat, trendy diet thing as a show for solidarity. Her coworker, more body conscious than Raquel, recently had a baby and was trying to lose the extra. Raquel had her sporadic tendencies, and this wasn't short of such an endeavor, but it was something that in the past she might not have done. She'd changed. The extremes to which they went had altered them both.

Alexander had just set his mind on possibly getting one more item from another truck when the wind picked up again. A feather floated by him and his eyes followed it to his left. There wasn't anything particular to his left except another line of people waiting to order food from another truck but there was something about the view that kept his eyes fixated. He didn't recognize her immediately. Her figure had not changed but her hair was different: slightly shorter, and burgundy. Just then she pulled it into a messy bun obviously tired of the wind having its way with it.

Without a doubt he knew it was Cashmere. She was wearing a Padres jersey but something about the way she looked in it made it seem as though it were on loan.

• • •

She hadn't noticed him. She was on her cell and it was good to know she still knew how to use one. Days after the last show he'd tried calling her, a week later he'd visited her and Emory's house but she'd already moved. Eventually out of desperation he tried to catch her at a MADD Maxi show. She'd quit. Her number had never changed. She just stopped. She never answered any of his messages and eventually her voicemail was full. Alexander was sure if he tried calling it now that it would still be in the same state.

He hadn't expected to see her. In fact, it'd seemed he'd spent time trying to figure out ways to accidentally bump into Cashmere before deliberately showing up to places like Emory's to confirm she had indeed moved; to Evan's house – where the band still gathered despite taking a hiatus, and more recently to a meeting with Trevor Colton.

"We're working the logistics now and would love for you to be involved."

Cashmere hadn't been there despite the hint that she might be. But now, here she was at one of the last outdoor concerts.

For all intents and purposes, it was a cold break. That night she'd arrived to some decision and whatever it was Alexander needed to do, that hadn't been done, triggered this reaction. That had been his assumption at least, he'd chosen wrong and while there was some truth to Cashmere's words Alexander still carried the fleeting moment of *something* that he still could not define. But was very much associated with her.

Right now there was no one standing between him and her. Without thought he'd gravitated toward her only slowing when he realized he had no idea what to say. Her back was to him and she seemed occupied by the call at hand. Or at least that was the effect she attempted to achieve, Alexander realized, when she accidentally gave herself away. It was in her posture. Something about it felt off.

There was a magnet that drew him. That gained steam once her lie was discovered. And without meaning to his hands, on auto-pilot, began to descend at her waist before his brain kicked in and his hand sought higher grounds and landed on her shoulder instead. Alexander expected Cashmere to startle but she hadn't, a deep sigh escaped instead. It felt heavy and one moment all stood still as Cashmere slowly turned to face him, dropping the act, she didn't say bye to her caller but simply slipped the phone into her back pocket.

"Finally noticed me, huh?" she said with a smile. Without warning she tipped onto her toes and wrapped Alexander into a tight embrace, "Chopped off all your hair I see."

"I think we've both made some alterations for our own reasons," Alexander said.

"Right. So," Cashmere started and cleared her throat, "This conversation can go several ways," she said as she moved up in the line. Alexander proceeded with her ignoring the dirty look of the person behind Cashmere.

"I'm not jumping," he said interrupting Cashmere.

"He's jumping, live with it," Cashmere countered just as quickly. The person mumbled a few colorful words and rolled their eyes but Cashmere was already linking her arm with Alexander's. "This could be a blip-- some odd universe coincidence that we actually ran into each other and just have some forced chit chat. We could catch up, as strained as it may be, and pretend I haven't been distancing myself from you."

"Or?"

"Does there have to be an 'or'? Maybe there should be an 'and' and we leave it at that, walk our separate ways, and forget each other again. Or try to."

"I haven't forgotten about you."

"I said try to."

"Is that what you've been doing? Trying to forget about me? I can tell you, from personal experience it's not everything you'd think it'd be. Especially when there are parts of you that remember..."

Cashmere looked up to the sky and closed her eyes against the brightness of the sun. A faint smile crept onto her lip before it vanished. "What happened Ernie?"

"What do you mean what happened? I'm still trying to piece together what I've done to-"

"Okay, let me rephrase, why do you think I did what I did?"

"You didn't want to be a puppet anymore; I get that but what I don't understand is why we-"

Cashmere shook her head. Alexander stopped. She cupped his chin, "Who are you here with Ernie?"

He paused and gave consideration to her question, suddenly hesitant to confirm what he suspected that she already knew. His mouth slightly opened but he couldn't find the will to let the name escape.

She smiled, "its okay."

"Who are you here with?" Alexander said quickly to be on the defense but Cashmere only gave him a slight smile. It was loaded. Her eyes crinkled at the corners and moisture was briefly there before she answered.

"No one."

Cashmere advanced in the line. Alexander still moved alongside her and even though they were in the same line it was as if they were propelling in two different lanes.

"I'm on a date with myself actually," Cashmere joked.

"No Art?"

She laughed, "No, no Art. No Dallas. No random guy lurking around the corner or keeping my seat warm. Just Cashmere."

Alexander wanted to say he couldn't believe it. Was glad to believe it but had trouble as his mind tried to process what it was Cashmere was saying but not saying.

"Neither of us were ready Ernie and I realized that when Emory came to me. Warning me about the show I'd be forced to do but I wouldn't have to because I already knew you'd stop it."

"Yes."

Cashmere smiled.

"I would," Alexander continued.

"But I didn't need your protection. I needed you to just be done. And you're still not there Ernie. You're still circling in this continuous loop of obligation unable to breakaway. In some ways, I am too," she whispered. Alexander barely caught the last part as the audience roared in the back. He'd forgotten about the concert.

"The fact that you're here with Raquel proves my point. I'm not better than you, not when I was putting on a show myself."

"But now you aren't? And how do you even know I'm here romantically with Raquel? We could just be here as friends?" Alexander was agitated. He knew his tantrum was nothing short of a four-year-old in a grown man's body as he tried to deny Cashmere's observations.

Cashmere stepped away from him and intertwined their fingers, she brought his hand to her lips and kissed the ring on his finger. She said nothing. They reached the booth to order and Cashmere let go of his hand, motioning for him to order first she then placed her order and paid for both.

They fell into silence as they stood waiting for their food to come back. Alexander wasn't ready. He wasn't ready for this to be goodbye.

Their food arrived and they slowly walked away from the truck. Cashmere stopped to face Alexander.

"And this is where I leave you."

"Cass," Alexander started, "I get it. And I know how this looks but I don't want this to be it. Can't we at least, just... I don't know. But it hardly seems fair that you based your decision on an 'us' on some arbitrary gesture."

"It wasn't. And it still isn't. First step is recognizing there's a problem and acknowledging it," she smiled. "Ernie for so long you've let a lot of things, people dictate your decision rather than this," she said poking at his heart. "And someday you'll want it to lead you places but today isn't that day. Maybe you'll remember someday..."

A tender smile broke across her face as she leaned in for a side hug, "See you around," she said as she walked off in the opposite direction. She never turned around, even as Alexander stood watching her. Watching her walk away, he realized then how he stood still.

She was gone.

He was unmoved. The food in his hand. The breezed swayed. The people that hustled and bustled around him. Everything around him was in motion. Ready. Moving. Taking the lead.

He stood still.

To himself, Alexander recognized, acknowledged, and admitted, "I'm not ready."

But someday I will be, he thought to himself as he walked back, returning to Raquel.

As Cashmere walked back toward her blanket in the grass, an arm wrapped around her shoulder.

"THAT WAS AMAZING! Dan tell me you got all that," Trevor said turning to the person to his left. "Gawd, this is going to be so good. Just back from the Midwest and already the love fever is stoked. We're going to have quite the time documenting all this Cashmere."

It hadn't felt real, but she found the muscles in her mouth as they began to form a semblance of a smile.

The solution lies in the problem she reminded herself. She was going to work through this.

It was going to be okay.

Finally, she was ready.

Acknowledgements

As I write this, I wonder, when had I started the first draft of TSP. Was it truly 2016? It makes sense based on the film reference but another part of me finds it difficult to believe that the year I managed to write my lightest, didn't go dark, story was also the same year someone important to me transitioned. This story was one, of many, attempts to write a love story, a romance. It's the closest I've gotten to one [for now]. The original ending was finite, in that it ended on a note of self-love, which to me offers up a new way of looking at romance. A return to loving one self. The ultimate gesture of acceptance... perhaps? But was it really complete? There was part of me that suspected there was more to Cashmere's story...

And for that reason. I have to thank friends that challenge me (often without them knowing). To my OWHP writing group- thank you for being there. To my friends that check in and show their support, I thank you. To the strangers I've met in passing, thank you for unknowing contributions... I am thankful for each day.

To the women that raised me. I don't think I can ever stop thanking you. For those that are still here and those that aren't, I carry each teaching, each lesson, as part of my life's toolkit. There is strength in numbers. I am surrounded in the love you've shown me. And the ways you still do even if some of you are no longer physically here... These tears are my love letter to you.

About the Author

Denise M. Jones, soon-to-be NYT Bestseller (she's speaking this into the universe), is a St. Louis Native that enjoy people watching. When not outing herself as nerdy or weird she can be found whispering to the novels in her drawer. She's currently holding them hostage, for their own protection.

Denise is working on releasing another Adult Children's book as well as the sequel to TSP.

Denise currently occupies space on her website:
www.denisemarquithjones.com

Denise's books: https://www.denisemarquithjones.com/books

Check her out on the following platforms if she hasn't deleted her account:
Twitter: @JonesMarquith
Facebook: https://www.facebook.com/dmjones.zeauthor
Instagram: https://www.instagram.com/denisemarquithjones/?hl=en

Winter Release Preview

"The Three Year War"

Chapter 1

Tasha Mason-D had three parents: A mother, a father, and a sperm donor. For them, there was only Tasha, and according to her mother there would only be her. It was also Tasha's mother that had once told Tasha that having three parents as an only child meant she was well loved. Except that had been a lie. Tasha valued many things, honesty the most, and out of all her mother's well-intentioned lies that one had always hurt the most. Still Tasha respected her family and abstract sentiments like loyalty, truth, and honor even when she herself fell short. Her situation unfolded a different sort of narrative that led her to live absent of such ideals. This truth had been one of the many warring thoughts inside Tasha's mind as she hid beneath the iron bed.

Tasha tried for quiet deep breaths. She aimed to slow her heartbeat, relax her mind, and loosen the muscles that strained with tension. It was for naught because at the slight instance of a creak the chatter began, her heart sped, and important thoughts eased forward without effort.

Tasha couldn't account for two of her parents. She bit her nails whenever her mind wandered at what could've possibly become of them as the result of the *one* parent. Despite all the many theories that trickled through her mind, cooled her veins, and watered her eyes the thing painfully clear was *Steve's not lucid.*

Tasha tried to rationalize with herself, understanding that even if there was the outstanding question of her mother's and Raj's whereabouts. There was the throbbing pain from her arm that screamed for attention. The false hope that maybe if she weren't injured and she could be quick and if Steve weren't out of medicine that maybe, *just* maybe, she might be able to convince him to take the meds or overpower him and shoot him up. Her mind wandered back to two of her parents, given Steve's state, she couldn't put anything past what he might do if he felt threatened, and for the first time Tasha gave consideration that her parents might be in the vault.

"Papa," Tasha whispered a broken sob. Her limbs shivered just as the floorboards groaned, the steps bent against its climber's will. Tasha had trouble remembering why she'd come back. Things were fine in the Wasteland. She had No and hung with Bee. Her life was filled. She wasn't alone. She was accepted amongst her sparse unusual world but her mother had been insistent for months, wanting Tasha to return home, promising things had gotten better.

Things hadn't. Tasha recognized a difference in Steve the moment she stepped through the door. He was too welcoming and he'd acknowledged her as a human and not as a thing to be ignored. It was too good to be true. He'd never liked her. From the very first moment she appeared on his doorstep, her hands clutched to her mother, his eyes narrowed to slits that day. They never opened wide again.

Until today.

Tasha hoped the AI-one wouldn't show. She closed her eyes and re-imagined the meeting date. It wouldn't be today. *It wasn't today.* Her coming home was only a coincidence. It wasn't an attempt to come back home, as her mother had wanted, and certainly wasn't to meet the person who held the key to her draft into the War.

Please don't let Bee show up. Please don't let Bee show up.

A horn blew. It was illegal to own any kind of mobile transportation within Folly. It was considered treason and because it was so, the only person bold enough to defy this would be Bee.

Tasha's brain seized. In her mind she saw Bee, parked off in the backyard drumming impatient fingers against the steering wheel, pushing forward the hair of a fresh short cut, it needed to be ruffled. That was Bee. Bee frustrated. Bee as s/he wore a path into the grass. Bee at the door, face twisted in a scowl, and then answered with a not so lucid knife wielding Steve.

Steve had just made it to the room Tasha was in when the horn stopped him. He stopped for several minutes, sniffled, and then a knock came at the door. Tasha's mind pulsed with added worry. Bee, despite much impatience, and Tasha's frenzied imagination, would not knock on the door.

Please don't be No Aw. Please don't be No Aw. Please don't be No Aw.

The dust stirred as Steve raced down the steps. The whole house felt the momentum and Tasha wept. What could she do? No Aw, Steve wouldn't know what to do with, the miscommunication would find them easy, there could be nothing understood if these two came together. No Aw and his limited speech. Steve lost to his darkness. He was having a moment and there was no helping it. From the start he'd been classified as "D" when really Steve was an "X".

Tasha heard the door open and slowly began to slide from underneath the bed. If it were different, if it had been Bee, Bee would do something. Bee was older. Bee had lived through much more than Tasha ever had, all she ever did was try to survive. At that moment, for Tasha, this meant continuing to hide even at the cost of losing one of the few things she held dear. She wished she'd listened more to the Fanatics. Maybe she'd know how to pray; instead she and Bee robbed their stock piles. Bee left a "thank you" note.

"Who are you!? Are you the getaway driver? Where's your car?" Steve yelled as he answered the door.

Tasha pictured him holding the knife to No Aw's neck. His eyes wide and lips trembling as he answered, "No Aw, No, Aw."

"I'm sorry," a different voice answered, hesitant. Tasha slid back under the bed, her arm shouted in protest. "Is this the Mason-D? I'm looking for a Tasha," the female voice said with authority.

AI-one. No, no, no, I closed my eyes, it wasn't today. It wouldn't be today.

"There's a burglar here," Steve answered. "A girl."

There was silence before the AI-one answered, "Mason-D? Are you a Mason-D? Is this the Mason-D?"

There was an accent, Tasha observed Mason-D sounded more like 'may san day' when the AI-one spoke. *Don't let him know*, Tasha wished. There were far worse things in her book, not making the War draft this round would be okay, hard, but manageable but spending the next five years elsewhere due to reclassification made her heart quicken as she held tight to her breath.

Don't let him know.

"I need her gone," Steve answered. "I think I got her. She's still inside."

"Sir," the AI-one started, "What is your name and classification?"

"I think she's in my daughter's bedroom. She's come to kill my family. They've sent her for what I've done. I have to get her."

"Sir," the AI-one answered as the steps thundered to life. "SIR!" Another set of feet rattled the steps just as Steve reached the top.

The horn blew again.

The steps stopped.

"Do you have a mobile sir," AI-one asked but Steve had only stopped long enough to observe the sound. He continued onward to the bedroom. Tasha heard the steps creak as someone went down them. The sound faded away. It exited the house. The horn sounded again but just as quickly as it came it stopped abruptly.

Bee.

Tasha began to tell herself this was just a dream. A dream she would wake from. A dream that was now a nightmare, one where she was being slid out from under the bed, hands that gripped so tight it cut the circulation off at her ankle, eyes pierced her, and a knife pointed to her chest.

This is it.

"Is this about her? Is it?" Steve said, the knife nicked Tasha's skin.

She didn't answer. The wrong one could get her killed and would only agitate him. She'd seen it before.

"What have you done to them?" Again the knife dug a little bit more. An explosion burst through the air, Steve turned to the sound and Tasha took a chance. She punched him in the jugular. The knife scratched the surface as she slid from underneath him and jumped over the banister. She slid over a few steps before she found purchase. Pain shot through her leg. Her arm festered but it was now more like a dull whine as she hobbled forward.

Tasha couldn't run. She didn't see the AI-one agent. She hadn't got what she'd come for. It was all a waste. She began to walk to the back of the house; Bee always came through the alley. Just as Tasha rounded the corner of the house, she felt herself dragged down. Her body flopped over limp, "WHO ARE YOU?! Who are you!?"

Tasha thought about answering but she couldn't speak. She could barely breathe. Spots decorated her vision. Her windpipe, choked by Steve's hand as his eyes stared. He was maddened by an idea that Tasha, since the first day, was an evil *thing*. An evil that Steve would rid the world of today; finally he'd have his way.

"Who are you!"

I'm your daughter.

"Who?!"

Please don't.

Tasha's hand went limp. She gathered the last bit of her strength and reached out to Steve. Not in a tender's daughter's caress as he squeezed the life from out of her but as a vengeful girl that'd never been loved. She dug her fingers into his skin, clawed at the idea of flight. It naturally kicked in, maybe one of few gifts she'd gotten from Steve. Or so Tasha thought. She had no way of...

Things faded quickly. Her eyes rolled back. She thought she heard another gun shot as a weight lifted from her chest.

"What are you doing?"

"That's your... our ..." Raj's voice broke.

Papa.

As Tasha's mind drifted, if she survived this she wouldn't come back. Bee had been right. Life was easier if she just let the idea go. Let them go. No one deserved this kind of life, not even as a resident of Folly. Tasha would be thirteen in another week. There wouldn't be a celebration this year. She had no reason to come back, not anymore.

A baby wailed nearby, somewhere in the distant depth of Tasha's mind, she registered the sound.

Please don't be...

www.ingramcontent.com/pod-product-compliance
Lightning Source LLC
Chambersburg PA
CBHW050417260626
47156CB00003B/1047